For My Brother

by

John C. Dalglish

2012

For My Brother

Prologue

Donnie Jarvis stepped off the school bus with his friend Tim Brown, and waved at the driver. The sixth grade boys lived just three houses apart in their South San Antonio neighborhood. The day was warm, but not uncomfortable, as the two boys turned for home.

They cut across the corner of Mr. Lander's perfect green lawn. The twelve-year-olds played a game almost every day with the retired man. Could they get across without him seeing? If he was outdoors, he would yell at them to get off the grass; if he was indoors, he'd pound on the large glass window overlooking the manicured lawn. Today was a win for them—he wasn't watching.

Tim hit Donnie lightly across the chest.

"Hey, what's all that about?"

Donnie looked up to see what had

caught his friend's attention. At the end of the block, in front of Donnie's house, was a chaotic scene. Blue and red lights lit up the fading afternoon light, reflecting off windows, signs, and cars. Yellow tape stretched across the front yard, wrapped around the big oak on the corner of the lot, and down along the side yard to the back fence. People, most in uniforms, were going in and out of his house like ants.

"I don't know..." Donnie's voice trailed off as fear took hold of him.

Instantly, he began running. His heart beat wildly in his chest, throbbing in his ears, as his feet pounded the pavement toward home. The closer he got to his house, the wilder the scene became. Donnie's neighbors stood at the edge of the yellow tape, some crying, others in small groups, talking and pointing at the house. It seemed as if every head turned toward him as he ran up.

Donnie stopped at the edge of the crime tape as still another police car, with lights flashing, rolled up to the scene. The passenger door swung open before the car even stopped, and Donnie's mom flew out of the car. Rushing toward the house, tears streaming down her face, she was stopped when she got to the front door. A man in plain clothes barred her from entering.

"Billy! Billy!" She tried to see over the man blocking her way. "Let me by!"

Donnie watched as the man held his mother in a bear hug while he spoke into her ear. She shook her head violently back and forth, as if trying to force the words out of her head.

"No. Nooooo!"

She slumped against the man, and he had to hold her tightly to keep her from collapsing on the walkway.

"Mom!"

His mom straightened up at the sound of Donnie's voice, searching for where his voice had come from. When she spotted him, she broke loose from the man, ran to Donnie, and wrapped her arms around him.

"Donnie! Are you okay?"

"Yeah. What's going on? Why are all these policemen here?"

His mother's face was drawn, almost gray. Pain welled up in her eyes, and Donnie realized he had seen that look before. It was the last time their world had crashed around them, the last time tragedy had visited their home just two years ago, when his dad passed away. That connection scared him even more, and he started to cry.

His mother brushed his tears away as she searched for words.

"Something has happened to Billy. There's been an accident."

Billy was Donnie's seventeen-year-old brother, and Donnie worshiped him. Billy, a senior in high school, would keep an eye on Donnie after school until their mom got home from work. They would throw a football around or play video games, and Billy never complained that it took time away from his social life.

"What happened? Is he okay?"

"No. I'm afraid he's not okay."

She paused, seemingly gathering strength for what she was about to say.

"Billy is dead."

She stared at him, and Donnie could tell she was waiting. Waiting to see how he reacted, what he would say, expecting him to scream. But he didn't react at all. Instead, life suddenly stood still for Donnie.

The words 'Billy is dead' bounced around the walls of his soul, looking for, but not finding, some place to take hold. Some place that could understand, and let the truth settle inside him. But he refused to let the words be part of him, to take root.

Tim walked up with the book-bag Donnie had dropped, and Donnie acted as if it was just another day.

"Oh thanks, Tim. I probably won't be at school for a few days."

"Okay..." His friend glanced at Donnie's mother, then back at his friend. "See ya later."

****

Donnie sat on the grass with his mother as the house slowly cleared of personnel. He had seen the body bag containing his brother wheeled out on a stretcher, and watched as it was loaded into a coroner's van, before being driven away. Most of the police cars had gone, one by one shutting off their lights and driving off into the early nightfall.

The yellow crime tape, now sagging toward the ground, still flapped in the breeze. It swayed unattended, no longer needed to hold onlookers at bay. The neighbors had returned to their homes to watch the evening news and look for themselves on TV.

The man in plain clothes who had blocked his mother's path, was a detective. It turned out there had been four people in the room with Billy. He brought each one of the kids outside and asked them the same questions.

Donnie sat nearby, listening intently as Billy's friends recounted what had happened in his brother's final moments.

He recognized two of them. Billy's best friend, Ed Garland, and Billy's girlfriend, Suzanne Cooper. The other two Donnie had never seen before. They told the detective their names were Dexter Hughes and Chelsea Burt.

Both girls were crying while the boys each wore a stunned, almost vacant look. Donnie wasn't crying; he was listening.

His brother's friends described a game called 'Russian Roulette.' Billy had spun the chamber of the gun, put it to his head, and pulled the trigger. Donnie couldn't understand what kind of game could involve shooting yourself. They said no one else had taken a turn; only his brother.

Donnie was listening to the fourth account when his mom finally realized what her son was hearing. She took him into the backyard.

They sat at the picnic table, and someone brought them each a cold soda. Donnie looked at his mother, her eyes red from crying, and it dawned on him they were alone. It was just the two of them now.

"What are we gonna do, Momma?'

"I don't know, Donnie. I don't know."

Chapter 1

"Donnie, it's time!"

Donnie Jarvis shut down his computer and pushed back his chair.

"Coming!"

He stopped at the bottom of the stairs to take a quick look in the mirror. Brown eyes stared back at him as he ran his hand through black hair, which never seemed to lie down in the same place twice. His t-shirt was clean, as were his jeans.

When he reached the top of the stairs, his mother was waiting for him in her wheelchair. Diabetes had taken its toll on her health, her legs in particular, and walking even short distances was difficult. She gave him a sideways glance.

"Let me look at you."

He posed for her as her eyes swept him up and down.

"Well, you're clean anyway. What

9

are you doin' downstairs all day?"

"Just playing on the computer. You ready to go?"

"Yes."

It was Sunday, and for the past ten years, Sunday meant a visit with Billy at the cemetery. If the weather was good, like it was today, they would spread a blanket out and sit for hours. His mother would chatter on telling Billy the latest news and who was doing what to whom in her soaps. She was always happiest when they were with Billy.

Of course, she never heard Billy speak back to her. It was just her way of staying connected to her oldest son. Donnie on the other hand, did have a connection with his brother. They did speak, and they had a plan. He headed for the door.

"I'll pull the van around."

Donnie went out through the back door to the garage. The white, metal building had two parking bays, but they only used one. Parked inside was the blue Chevy Astro. Even though the car was old and ugly, his mother could manage getting in and out of it better than most cars. Donnie had sold his Chevy Impala when his momma couldn't drive anymore. He just took to driving the van.

He backed out and drove around front where his mother was waiting on the porch. Getting out, he helped her stand so she could get hold of the rail. She struggled, taking one step at a time, down from the porch to the side door of the van. When Donnie had her settled in the passenger's seat, he returned to the porch, folded the wheelchair, and loaded it in the back of the van. One day he hoped to get her an automatic chairlift.

Climbing back into the driver's seat, down the farm lane. "Nice day for our visit, Momma."

"It is. I so enjoy our time together as a family. A day like this makes it all the nicer."

The driveway was a quarter-mile dirt trail leading out to the county road. Their home, an old farmhouse on seven acres, was located ten miles east of San Antonio. It's white with a green roof and a matching garage. An old barn sat on the property, appearing to defy gravity in its effort to remain standing. It used to be white as well, but hadn't been painted in years.

They'd moved here right after Billy died. In fact, neither Donnie nor his mother, had gone back inside their house following his brother's death. His mother had enlisted a real estate friend to clean up, and then sell it. They didn't get much for it, just wanted enough to leave the memories behind. She had used some of the money to pay for the funeral, and the rest to buy the farm.

"I made us some iced tea to enjoy while we visit."

Donnie hadn't noticed the bottle in the huge sack she called her purse, but there it was along with some Styrofoam cups. "That'll be nice."

The cemetery was just a few minutes from home, and they arrived just after three in the afternoon. Donnie turned the Astro onto the driveway leading into the 'Gates of Heaven Memorial Cemetery.'

A fifteen-minute drive on I-10, east from San Antonio, the small rural cemetery relied on donations to keep the grass mowed and the gates from falling down.

As usual, they were the only ones there. He followed the dirt track to the rear, then around to the west, before stopping in front of several stones indicating the final resting place of the less fortunate.

Donnie had seen some of the nice cemeteries in the city, the ones he and his mother hadn't been able to afford. Despite the name, 'Gates of Heaven' was a far cry from what his brother deserved.

He removed her wheelchair from the van and put it where she could get into it. Holding her arm to steady her, he got her seated, and pushed her over to Billy's grave. He parked her where she could reach the headstone, and she leaned over to brush the leaves away from her son's name. Once satisfied with her housekeeping, she laid a single red rose across the stone.

"Hi, Billy. I missed you this week."

Donnie watched as his mother carried on the conversation. His mother had never heard Billy, she just pretended.

Donnie's relationship with his older brother was different. He could hear Billy. Not on these visits with his mother, but when he came on his own so they could make their plans.

Today, Donnie would watch, drink tea, and enjoy his mother's smiles as she shared with Billy. He would return alone tonight, after dark, when he could hear the voice of his brother clearly. They had further plans to make, and Donnie sensed something big was coming. He hoped Billy would tell him soon.

Today's visit was short; they had

been there just ninety minutes when his mother turned to him.

"I'm ready to go."

She looked back at the grave.

"Bye, Billy. See you next week. Love you."

****

When they arrived home, Donnie helped Momma back into the house, parked the van, and started back to the basement.

"Don't you want dinner, Donnie?"

"No. I'll make a sandwich later."

Shutting the door behind him, he descended the stairs. Switching his computer on, the password request window loaded up. He typed in 'Brothers.' A file popped up with the names of four people listed across the top. Donnie clicked on the first name. Suzanne Cooper.

Another screen opened with a full biography of his brother's former girlfriend. One of the first tasks Billy had given him, in their early talks, was to start a file on each person present the day of the Russian roulette game.

Donnie had made notes on each of them during their talks. Billy told him what to look into, what information he wanted, and how to find all four people.

It had taken Donnie several years, but as he improved with his computer, he got better at finding information.

Using social networks and identity searches to build each file, he now had the address, family relations, work place, and much more, for each person on his list. Billy had been proud of how well he'd done gathering the information.

Billy had not given him his mission yet, but Donnie could already feel the time was coming when action would be necessary. He looked forward to it.

He stared at the face of the girl on the screen. Would she be first in Billy's plan, or would it be one of the others? Donnie was sure he would know soon.

Chapter 2

The sun had set by the time Donnie returned to the cemetery. His mother usually questioned him about where he was going, and he always said the same thing.

"Just gonna hang with a friend."

He would be out the door before she could ask who the friend was.

For many, a cemetery was no place to be after dark, but Donnie loved the solitude. It allowed him to hear his brother, and his brother to hear him. They were never interrupted in the cemetery at night.

"Hi, Billy."

Donnie stood looking down at the rose his mother had left. The petals were bathed in waning moonlight, and he stared at it without seeing, listening intently for his brother's voice.

"Billy, I need to know what the next step in our plan is. I've got the files complete and updated, just as you asked, but I'm sure there's more I could be doing."

Donnie started nodding his head up and down.

"Okay."

He reached into his pocket, pulled out a pencil along with some scrap paper, and began to draw. In the low moonlight, his crude picture was hardly recognizable, but he felt he knew what Billy was saying.

"I understand, Billy. I'll begin immediately."

He finished the drawing and looked back from the paper toward his brother's name on the stone.

"No, I won't tell Mom. It's just between us."

He tucked the pencil back in his jeans and folded the sheet of paper up, sliding it into a shirt pocket.

His face turned sad. It always did when the time came to leave his brother.

"I gotta go, Billy. I'll be back in a few days. Miss you."

Donnie turned and walked slowly, head down, back to his car. He always looked forward to visiting his brother, but each visit tore at him, overwhelming him with sadness. It never got easier.

He started his car and turned it toward the exit.

****

"Where have you been?"

"I told you, Momma. You know you don't have to worry about me."

She was sitting in her chair watching 'America's Funniest Videos.' She'd seen the same episode a dozen times, but she stilled laughed at the same clips. Donnie kissed her on the top of her head; she was not appeased.

"You're either off running around or hiding in the basement. I don't know the names of any of your friends, we never talk about your outings, and you never keep your mother company anymore."

"Oh come on, Momma. I'm twenty-two and there's things to do, people to see, worlds to conquer."

She refused to smile at his joke.

"I never see any friends come over, and the phone doesn't ring. Whose worlds are you conquering?"

Donnie laughed and started for the stairs to the basement.

"Where you goin'?"

"Downstairs. I've got something I

need to do before going to bed."

His mother made a pouty face as she turned toward the TV. Donnie smiled to himself. She couldn't stay mad at him. He hurried down the stairs, excited by the new task.

With his computer open, he made a new file. He typed the name 'Containment' in the description line. He prepared the file, so he could enter the data as each measurement was taken.

Donnie needed to get the drawing Billy had given him onto the computer while it was still fresh in his mind.

Taking a tape measure, he stretched it the length of the basement. The measurement went into the file. Next, he stretched it crossways in the room. That measurement entered, he found the available square footage in the room. He subtracted the space he needed for his desk, divided the result by four, giving him the final size.

He smiled to himself. Four-foot-by-eight-foot would be the size of each cell. It was easy for him to envision the layout, and he spent the next hour making a materials list for the project. It had to be done right, and it had to be strong. Billy was counting on him.

For My Brother

****

The next morning, Donnie was up early getting ready for work. He had a part-time job with Summit Construction. He couldn't work full time because he needed to be around for his mother, but the extra money helped to supplement her disability check.

Mostly, his job was to 'gopher' for the full-time guys. The work was spotty, and physically demanding, but he was looking forward to going this morning.

"Bye, Momma. I'll see you later."

He kissed her forehead, as he always did before he left, and rushed out the back door.

"Wait! When you comin' home?"

He didn't hear her; he was already in the garage getting into the van.

Donnie arrived at the job site about twenty minutes later. Summit was building a condominium complex in the northeast suburb of Windcrest. He found his boss in the site trailer.

"Morning, Gary."

"Hi, Donnie. You ready to get to work?"

"Yes, sir."

"Okay, I need you running wheelbarrows of gravel up to Smitty and

Dixon. They're prepping the sidewalk from Building One to the parking lot."

"Yes, sir."

Donnie left the trailer and went to find the wheelbarrow. He knew he was in for a long day hauling gravel was hard work, but lunchtime would give him an opportunity to focus on his real mission for the day.

****

After a long, hot morning, Donnie took lunch with the rest of the guys, but he didn't eat with them. Smitty saw him leaving.

"Where you goin'?"

"Gotta run an errand."

"Better be back in an hour."

"I will."

Donnie got in his van, drove around the block, and parked just out of sight of the office trailer. Leaving the van running to use the air conditioning, Donnie waited for his boss to leave.

Gary Maddox took lunch downtown with his girlfriend, and Donnie planned to use the time his boss was gone to sneak into the site office.

Gary kept a .38 caliber revolver, which he called the 'Texas Deal Maker,' in an unlocked desk drawer. Donnie had seen the gun dozens of times, every time Gary told his favorite story.

He would pull the gun out of the drawer, show it to the latest visitor, and then tell the same story.

"Some guy who worked for me said I cheated him out of a day's pay. He was wrong, of course, but he refused to leave the job site. I got this gun, and went out to talk with him.

I said, 'This is called the Texas Deal Maker, and I'm going to use it to make you a deal. You leave now, and I won't use it.'

He didn't move, so I asked him if he was married, and he said, 'Yeah, so what?'

So I said, 'If you don't leave now, I'm gonna have to change the name of this gun to Texas Widow Maker.' He left."

At that point, Gary would laugh as if it was the first time he'd told the story.

Donnie thought it was funny the first couple of times, but the story had lost its charm. Nonetheless, he knew it meant that a lot of people knew where that gun was, and that worked to his advantage.

A few minutes after he parked,

Donnie watched his boss's gray Dodge truck leave the construction site. He shut the van off, and climbed out.

Checking his watch, he stepped through a gap in the fence, and came around from behind the trailer. After making sure no one had seen him, he slipped into the office.

A blast of cool air hit him as he shut the door. Avoiding the windows, he walked over to the desk and slid the drawer open. The gun sat where he expected it to be. Picking it up, he opened the chamber. It was loaded. He clicked the chamber shut, and stuffed it down the front of his pants.

Moving quickly back to the door, he cracked it open. The sound of tires on gravel stopped him cold.

Was it his boss back early? Did Gary forget something?

Donnie could put the gun back, and get it another day. However, he knew he might lose his nerve if there had to make a second attempt.

He waited, and the sound of a vehicle turning around started his heart beating again. When it left the lot, he stuck his head out. He didn't see anyone, and quickly retraced his steps to the van.

Once inside, he hid the gun under

his seat and started the vehicle. He still had an errand to run.

****

"You're late!"

"Am not! Got ten minutes left."

Donnie smiled. He knew the guys liked to give him a hard time, and he wasn't late. He set his Burger King bag down, and pulled out a hamburger.

"So Donnie, what was your errand?"

Donnie reached into his back pocket, pulled out new set of work gloves, and held them up for everyone to see.

"Just needed new gloves."

Smitty grinned.

"Hands hurt? Must be getting soft, Donnie."

"Not soft, just working harder than you, and wearing my old gloves out."

Donnie smiled to himself. His old gloves were fine, laying in his van, but the guys ribbing him meant no one had seen him. He'd accomplished his mission for the day.

Billy will be pleased.

Chapter 3

Donnie pulled off the county road and headed down his lane. Getting the gun had pumped him up, and he looked forward to telling Billy. His brother would be proud of him, and would want to know all the details of this milestone in their plans.

In the distance, he could see Momma waiting on the porch. She liked to roll herself out and wait for Donnie to come home from work. Many times, she would have a glass of cold tea waiting for him, and he would sit next to her as they watched the sun go down.

Donnie had wanted to share the plan his mother, but Billy had reacted badly to the idea. On one of his late night visits, he had asked permission, and his brother had been very clear how he felt. Donnie had been surprised by the response.

Whenever Donnie recalled the

conversation, it was with some sadness. He couldn't remember a time when Billy was alive that he'd ever gotten that angry with him.

He didn't like Billy getting mad at him. It didn't happen often, but it always left Donnie upset.

Sometimes Donnie would catch Momma dozing when he drove up, and today was one of those days. He thought about blowing the horn to wake her, but she probably wouldn't think it was funny.

Stopping the van in front of the porch, he climbed out. Climbing the steps to where she sat, he touched his mother on the shoulder.

"Momma?"

She didn't move. He shook her a little harder.

"Momma?"

She didn't respond. He bent down in front of her, his heart pounding, and looked up into her face. It was gray.

"Momma! Momma!"

Donnie shook her harder, and her head rolled back. He put his hand on her throat to check for a pulse. She was cold. He fell back onto the porch, tears rolling down his face.

"Oh…Momma."

****

Donnie didn't know how long he'd been sitting at his dead mother's feet, but the sun was disappearing over the horizon when he finally decided what to do. Actually, he decided what not to do.

He didn't call 911. Instead, he decided to talk to his brother.

Billy would tell him how to handle his mother's death and what the impact would be on their plan.

Donnie wheeled his mother back inside and into her bedroom. Cradling her in his arms, he managed to get her onto the bed. He gently laid her out, crossed her hands on her chest, and covered her up. Leaning over, he kissed her on the forehead.

"I love you, Momma; I always will."

He turned off the light and closed the bedroom door.

He hadn't eaten, so he grabbed a bottle of chocolate milk from the fridge, and went back out to the van. He needed to get to the cemetery, needed to get to Billy, and receive some guidance.

He knew his mother's death would accelerate their plan, and he needed to focus on something other Momma.

The moon was new and the cemetery dark when he arrived. Parking in his usual spot, he got out and slowly walked to his brother's grave. He was dreading the news he had to deliver.

"Hi, Billy. It's me. I've got some sad news."

Donnie stood quietly looking down at his brother's name. The rose his mother left lay wilted, dying. Donnie's heart broke as he bent down, picked it up, and twirled it in his fingers. He could see his Momma there, laying it on the stone, and his tears began to fall once more.

His expression changed from sad to surprised as a voice no one else could hear spoke to him.

"You already know?"

He listened.

"You knew it was coming?"

More silence.

"Why didn't you tell me? Why didn't you warn me?"

Donnie was angry. His brother could have prepared him. Instead, he chose not to, and Donnie couldn't understand why. His brother refused to tell him, changed the subject.

Donnie scowled. "Yeah, I got it. It went without a hitch."

Donnie didn't really want to discuss

the plan. He needed to know what to do about Momma. He needed to know things would be okay.

Donnie sensed the loss of his mother could be the catalyst for getting Billy his final rest, but he also feared it might derail everything. Right now, Donnie knew he needed the mission to keep his life from unraveling.

"Where should I put Momma, Billy? There's no room for her here with you, and I don't want her far from us."

Donnie's eyebrows went up as he listened.

"Really? Do you think it would be alright?"

A smile came to Donnie's face. "That's an awesome idea! I'll take care of it now, but I'll be back soon. I love you, Brother."

****

The next morning dawned warm, and found Donnie up early. He went into the barn, gathered wood from the lumber pile, and laid it out on the ground.

He pieced it together in his mind. Some nails and he thought it would do the job.

Donnie was supposed to work again

today, and so he needed to call in. His boss answered.

"Hi, Gary. Momma's real sick, so I won't be able to work today."

"Okay."

Donnie sensed something wasn't right.

"I'll probably be in tomorrow morning."

"Fine. Donnie, you wouldn't know what happened to my gun, would you?"

Donnie's heart started to pound.

"Your gun? What gun? You mean the 'Deal Maker'?"

"Yeah, it's been stolen. You know anything about that?"

"No, of course not."

A moment of silence dragged on before his boss spoke again.

"Listen, I don't need the help right now, anyway. I'll let you know if I want you in the future."

The line went dead before Donnie could respond. He hung up the phone. He didn't want to lose his job, but he was relieved.

His boss doesn't know who took the gun.

He suspects me, but he doesn't know for sure. One less thing to worry about.

****

He worked on it for most of the day, and when it was done, he stood back to look it over. Donnie was pretty sure his brother would be impressed.

Donnie placed the lid on and carried the box to the house. Setting it down on the porch, he stopped for the night. He would finish the other half of his task tomorrow.

Going into the house, he washed up, made himself a sandwich, and sat down at the kitchen table. The TV was off, his mother being the only one who watched it, and the house was quiet.

The loneliness Donnie felt from the loss of his mother began to suffocate him. He was now completely isolated.

First Billy, and now Momma, had left him. He had no friends, no other family, and now no job. Just Billy, and the responsibility to help him rest. Sadness washed over him. It helped that he could still visit his brother, but it didn't stop the pain he felt inside.

Donnie got up and moved to the couch, lying down on his side. He closed his eyes, held his stomach, and began to moan. A physical pain in his chest made him rock back and forth, tears filling his eyes.

He didn't know how long he lay there, but after a while, Donnie wiped his sleeve across his face and got up. He needed to get out of the house, and decided now was as good a time as any to look for Momma's burial site.

Going out the back door and around the garage, he stood looking over the farm property. Trees lined the fencerow along the back of the property, and Texas scrub had grown up through both the east and west fences. There was a small rise behind the garage with a Blackjack oak towering above the whole property.

"You're gonna' rest there, Momma. Close to me, so I can visit anytime."

Knowing his mother would remain close by helped to calm the storm raging inside Donnie. He would bury her tomorrow, and then be ready to focus on the job he had to do for his brother.

Chapter 4

Donnie was up early again the next morning. The day promised to be hot, and the job ahead of him grueling. Toast and orange juice served as breakfast.

After filling a rinsed-out quart milk jug with cold water, he went to the barn.

Hanging on the wall was a pick, which he took down, and over in the corner was an old shovel. He examined the handle on the shovel and decided it needed reinforcement. Several wrappings of duct tape satisfied him that the shovel would hold up.

Walking out to the rise behind the garage, Donnie found himself in a surprisingly good mood. He had a job to do, an important one, and that always made him feel better. A task allowed him to focus, to close off emotion, to sweat out some of the pain in his life.

Donnie removed his shirt, tied it

around his head like a bandana, and made a mental rectangle in the dirt. Starting at the base of the rectangle, he plunged the pick into the dirt.

Once, twice, three, and then four times. He raised and plunged the pick into the dry Texas ground. Next, he took the shovel and removed the dirt he had broken loose.

Over and over, pounding the dirt, shoveling out his pain. It was slow, hot, tedious, but he needed it.

Donnie took frequent breaks, but was driven to keep going by the thought of helping his mother rest. She would be at peace on their land, and Donnie would be free to focus on finally bringing Billy peace.

By four in the afternoon, Donnie judged the hole to meet the needs of his mother's coffin. He sat in the shade of the oak, and drank from his third quart of water. It seemed to escape directly out through his pores as soon as he poured the water down his throat. He stayed in that spot until he felt strong enough to bring Momma out of the house.

He placed the box next to the grave with the lid leaning against it. Inside, he laid his Momma's favorite quilt and a needlework pillow, which had both her boys' names on it.

Donnie went inside to his mother's room, gathered her into his arms, and carried her out to where the box sat. As gently as he could, he laid her in the homemade casket. He pulled the quilt up around her, and put the pillow under her head.

Going over to the rose bush where she'd cut a rose each time she visited Billy, he clipped one for her, and laid it on her chest.

Staring down at her, the tears began again, as he prepared to place the lid over her. He would never see her face again.

After saying a small prayer, he willed himself to slide the lid over the box, and hammer in some nails to seal it.

Using some rope, he managed to lower the box into the hole. Taking the shovel, Donnie prepared to start pushing dirt back into the hole.

"Goodbye, Momma. I love you. I sure am going to miss you. Rest now."

Donnie shoveled dirt until after dark, covering the box completely. He sat down at the base of the grave, resting his head in his hands, while he stared at the fresh mound of dirt. It was done. Momma could rest.

For My Brother

****

The sun blinded Donnie as he rolled onto his back. Covering his face with his hand, he tried to figure out where he was. It took him a minute before he realized he'd fallen asleep at the foot of Momma's grave.

He got up and tried to stretch. Every muscle complained. He was sore from the work, but his mind felt refreshed.

He brushed himself off and went in the house. His stomach growled as he rummaged through the fridge looking for something to eat. A tub of plain yogurt with some maple syrup would have to do. After wolfing it down, he thought to look at the clock. He was surprised to see it was almost noon.

Donnie spent the remainder of the afternoon picking up the tools and cleaning around his mother's grave. Next, he made a cross, which he stuck in the ground by her head.

Finally, he took a flat board, and using his pocketknife, scratched his Momma's name. Under her name, he etched the dates of her birth and death.

He held it away from him and studied it.

It will do fine. Momma would like it.

He nailed it to the cross, and sat at the foot of the grave while he watched the sun sink behind the horizon. It reminded him of their evenings on the porch together.

He was glad she was close enough they could still share the sunset. When the light finally disappeared, and dusk started to turn to night, he stood.

"Goodnight Momma. I'm going to see Billy now."

****

Donnie sat on the ground by the stone with Billy's name.

"Hi, Billy. I did what you suggested. Momma is buried behind the garage. She'll not be alone there, and I can visit whenever I want. We watched the sunset together tonight."

Donnie smiled. "I'd like that, too. Maybe when we're done, I can have you moved next to Momma. I'm sure she would be happy to have you near."

The rose his mother had left several days before had blown into the grass. Wilted as it was, Donnie picked it up and put it back on Billy's gravestone.

"Okay, Billy. I understand. The rooms are the priority, and I'll work to have them done as quickly as possible. What should I put in each cell?"

Donnie nodded his head up and down several times.

"Got it. We'll have this done soon, and then you can rest. I can feel everything is going to be fine."

Donnie laughed aloud.

"Hey! This is different, and that was a long time ago. I won't make the same mistake again, not this time. I won't let the wrong person know what's going on."

Donnie glanced at his watch.

"I gotta go, Billy. There's a lot to do, and I need to pick up supplies. Love you. I'll be back soon."

Donnie turned and walked back to the van. He pushed the usual sadness away by focusing on the things he needed at the store. If he got them all tonight, he could start building first thing in the morning.

****

Donnie arrived at the Lowe's store on Goliad Street in Southeast San Antonio about 9:30. The store closed in half an hour, but he knew what he needed. With help from an employee, he managed to collect everything before the store closed.

He put his cartload on the checkout table.

Four padlocks, keyed the same. A large box of screws. Twelve pieces of one-foot-long steel rebar. Four pieces of chain, each three feet long. Four heavy eyebolts. Another package of four padlocks, also keyed the same. Five-gallon buckets with their lids, four of them. Four latches that accepted padlocks, and four thick moving blankets.

"Whatcha makin'?"

Donnie looked up, surprised by the question.

"Oh, it's a 4-H project for my son."

The cashier smiled at him while she rang him up.

"Cool. I was in 4-H. Loved it, but I don't remember any projects like this."

Donnie tried to remain calm. He didn't want to be noticed, never mind questioned.

"Well, you know how it is. Things change."

The cashier let it go, and gave Donnie his total. He was relieved to pay and get out the door.

There was an H-E-B Foods on his way home, where he stopped for some groceries, before heading back to the house. He eagerly anticipated the next morning, when he would be able begin the final steps of his mission.

His mind raced with the possibilities of the next step in the plan. Billy still hadn't shared what it was, but each time Donnie completed a new project, it brought him closer to the ultimate final step. Donnie couldn't wait to know what that step was.

****

Six straight days of hard work had brought Donnie to the end of his construction project. He had visited Billy about halfway through to make sure he was getting everything right. Billy had been pleased and told Donnie so.

It always meant a lot when his big brother was proud of him. Four solid cells were complete, and the final preparations were underway.

Donnie placed one of the five-gallon buckets in each cell. They would serve as toilets for the people inside. Each cell was made of wood from the pile in the barn. Solid oak frames with steel bars in the window of each door. A blanket on the floor of each room covered a chain coiled beneath it. The chains led to a large eyebolt, which Donnie had secured to the walls. Each door sat open with a padlock resting on the handle.

Donnie went to his computer, running down the names on his list. Four in all, each burned into his memory since that awful day.

Ed Garland, his brother's best friend. Suzanne Cooper, his brother's girlfriend. Dexter Hughes and Chelsea Burt. Two people Donnie had never seen before that day.

It was time to choose the first name, and Billy had left it up to him. His brother didn't care who was first, and Donnie had debated for a couple days before making up his mind. And now it was time.

Chapter 5

Detective Jason Strong was just leaving his Terrill Hills neighborhood when his cell phone rang. He turned onto the highway leading to the station before answering.

"Hello?"

"Hey, Jason. How's it going?"

It was Jason's partner, Vanessa Layne. She was on maternity leave, but was having a hard time not being involved with his investigations.

"Hey, Vanessa! Long time, no hear."

"Very funny. Just wanted to remind you I come back in a couple weeks. Are you on a case now?"

"Nope. Nina and I are just putting the final touches on the murder case from the nightclub. You remember the one I told you about *yesterday*."

Jason smiled into the phone. Nina

Jefferson had been his temporary partner since Vanessa's maternity leave started three months ago. She's a good cop, but Jason missed Vanessa as much as she missed working.

"Okay, okay. I get it. Just trying to stay in the loop."

Jason understood. "How's Kasen?"

The mention of her son perked her up. "Good! You and Sandy need to come visit him."

The thought of his partner's son always made Jason smile, as did the mention of Sandy.

Sandy was Jason's wife. They met in college at the University of Texas at Austin. She was finishing her teaching degree, and he was there attending the police academy. They had no kids of their own, but Jason could tell little Kasen has Sandy thinking about what color to put in a nursery. Jason heard a baby cry in the background.

"You bet. I'll get in touch with Sandy and we'll plan on coming over."

"Gotta run. Talk to you later." Vanessa hung up without waiting for an answer.

Jason laughed.

"I'm sure."

A few minutes later, he wheeled his

car into the station parking lot. The day was typical for late summer, hot with very little breeze, so the air conditioning was welcome relief as he came through the station doors. His long-time friend Dave Connor was at the sergeant's desk.

"Hi, Dave. How's Vicky?"

"Mean as ever! And Sandy?"

"Great. Thinking a little too much about babies. Nina in yet?"

Dave let out his big laugh. "Yeah, saw her a few minutes ago."

"Okay, thanks. See ya later."

Jason got on the elevator and pushed the third-floor button, making it glow. A few moments later, the elevator doors slid open with a ding. The entire third floor is Homicide.

His desk sat facing Vanessa's, the two pushed up against each other. Nina was sitting in Vanessa's spot when he walked up.

Black, short, stocky, with curly hair, she was the consummate officer. Jason had come to appreciate her calmness and professional demeanor when things got tense. Still, even after three months, he hadn't got used to seeing her in Vanessa's chair.

Jason had just pulled out his own chair when Lieutenant Patton stuck his head out of his office.

"You two, in here!"

The two detectives exchanged glances and headed into the office. Nina took a chair while Jason stayed standing, leaning on the doorframe. "What's up?"

Lieutenant John Patton was a big man; he works out even on his days off. Balding, but with bushy eyebrows and an unruly moustache, he claimed his hair was moving from his head to his face. When he was under stress, his eyebrows would knit together to form a hedge, which was apparently the case this morning.

He handed Nina a piece of paper.

"I don't like to do it, but the captain didn't give me any choice. I have to loan you two out."

"Where?"

"Downstairs."

Jason groaned.

"Why? What did we do to deserve this punishment?"

"It's not a punishment! You two are next up on the board, and so you get to help out our brothers."

Nina appeared less than thrilled as well.

"It's not a narcotics case, is it?"

"No. A simple missing persons

case. They're covered up and need an extra set of detectives. You're it. Go see Lieutenant Banks."

Jason and Nina headed to the elevator. On the way down to second floor, Nina asked what Jason knew about Lieutenant Banks.

"Well, I've never met her personally, but there are stories."

"Oh. What kinda stories?"

"Horror mostly."

Jason laughed, but Nina didn't seem amused. "Great!"

The elevator doors opened and they walked up to an officer at the front desk.

"Lieutenant Banks?"

A thumb jerked over a shoulder served as directions.

They found Lieutenant Sarah Banks standing behind her desk. Tall with close-cropped, dark brown hair and green eyes, she was an imposing figure. Jason had heard getting on her bad side was not a good idea.

They knocked on the door of her office, and she looked up. "Yes?"

Jason put on a bright smile. "Lieutenant Banks?"

"Yes?" She did not return his smile.

"Lieutenant Patton asked us to come down and see if we can help out.

I'm Detective Strong and this is Detective Jefferson."

"Perfect. I appreciate the help."

Still no smile as she rummaged around on her desk. Eventually, she found a file folder, and held it out to Jason.

"Missing person. Twenty-eight-year-old male. Address is on the second sheet. Golfing buddy reported him missing this morning. Uniforms are there and have the location secured."

Jason flipped the file open as Nina took notes on what the lieutenant was saying. Lieutenant Banks went back to what she was doing before they'd come in. After a few moments, the lieutenant looked up again.

"Is there something else?"

Jason looked at Nina. They shook their heads.

"Well, I don't know how it is in Homicide. Down here, when you're handed a file, you get going."

Nina and Jason exchanged glances, then beat a hasty retreat out the door. Back in the elevator, Nina did her best imitation.

"Well, I don't know how it is in Homicide…"

Jason laughed.

"She's all business, that's for sure."

"She's all something."

The elevator doors opened and they went to their desks. Nina got on her computer while Jason read through the file.

Ed Garland was a factory worker, had been at the same job for eight years, and lived on the west side. A uniformed officer had responded to the initial call for a missing person. Apparently, Mr. Garland didn't show for a golf date yesterday, and his friend hadn't been able to reach him in two days.

Nina looked up from the computer screen.

"No record. Valid driver's license."

"Okay. Let's go out to the house."

****

Donnie looked through the bars at his first 'guest.' Ed Garland sat on the blanket, one end of a padlocked chain wrapped around his leg and the other bolted to the far wall. He couldn't move more than about two feet in either direction.

Donnie unlocked the door. He carried a glass and a granola bar into the room.

"Here. Drink this protein shake and eat the granola bar."

Ed ignored the food.

"Why are you doing this? Why am I here?"

"Can't tell you yet. You'll find out soon enough."

Donnie could see the fear and confusion in Ed's face, and he felt for him, but there was no choice. Ed was just one of the necessary pieces for Billy's plan.

Donnie had to focus on the mission, not emotions. Especially now that he'd taken his first captive. He had to see it through.

"Just let me go. I won't tell anyone. Please."

Donnie left the food on the floor and exited the room. He closed the door behind him without saying anything more.

Padlock in place, he went over to his desk and turned on the computer. A file popped up of the next person he was to go after. Chelsea Burt, now Chelsea Morris.

The face on the screen looked back at him with a carefree smile. She had no way of knowing Donnie was coming, and he liked it that way.

The women are the hardest for Donnie—his momma had always taught him respect—but he would do what he had to. He closed the computer and headed up the stairs.

****

Jason and Nina pulled up at the address on the west side of the city. The neighborhood was run-down and tired-looking, the kind of area where people don't have the garbage cans by the house, but instead bring the garbage to the curb. More than one can had been knocked over, its contents scattered by hungry dogs.

Ed Garland lived in a small duplex with peeling, yellow paint and virtually no landscaping. The responding officer was still there, standing in front of Ed Garland's door. A man stood next to the officer, who Jason assumed was the golfing buddy.

"Nina, you want to see if you can learn anything from the neighbors?"

"Sure."

Jason walked up to the officer.

"Have we got access to the house?"

"Yes, sir. His friend here, Jerry Baker, had a key. When he found Mr.

Garland wasn't home, he called us. Mr. Baker stayed outside until I got here."

"Okay, good. Anybody else live with him?"

"No. An ex-wife lives here in town, and I spoke with her, but she claims to have had no contact with Mr. Garland in a couple months. Also, she apparently wasn't surprised to hear her ex was missing, but she wouldn't say why."

"Really? Okay, stay here while I take a look around."

Jason went up the walk and pushed the door open. In the living room, he found a half-eaten hot dog, and a partial glass of something that looked like milk.

He continued through to the kitchen and down a small hallway, glancing into the bathroom as he passed it. Everything seemed to be in order until he got to the back bedroom.

Jason noticed the window was cracked slightly open and the screen was missing. He went to the back door and found it unlocked. Outside, the screen lay on the ground below the window, next to a set of shoe prints in the soft soil below the ledge. He went back through the house and found the uniformed officer.

"Get on your radio and call for a forensic team. Tell them Detective Strong made the request."

"Yes, sir."

Jason turned to the friend.

"Jerry Baker, is it?"

"Yeah."

"When was the first time you noticed your friend wasn't around?"

"Two days ago. I called him to confirm our golf date, but got no answer. I left a message, but he didn't call back. Yesterday, I showed up to play golf and he wasn't there. I played with the two other guys in our group."

"I'd like you to give their names to the officer."

"Sure."

"So when did you decide to come over to the house?"

"I called him at work this morning, but they said he didn't show. So I left my job to come over and see what was up."

"And being out of contact for a couple days is unusual for you two?"

"Yeah. We've been friends for years, and he never misses work or golf without calling."

"Okay, thanks."

Jason saw Nina coming back down the sidewalk and went to meet her.

"Anything?"

She shook her head.

"Hear no evil, see no evil. Nobody admits to noticing anything."

"To be expected. Folks in this area tend to keep to themselves, at least officially."

She put her notebook away and looked at him.

"How 'bout you? You find anything?"

"Actually, I do want to show you something. Come take a look."

Nina followed him through the living room and into the bedroom, where he pointed at the windowsill.

"I think we may have a point of entry here. I called for a forensic team."

The uniformed officer stuck his head in the bedroom door. "Forensics is here."

"Okay, thanks."

A few minutes later, the tech came into the back of the house.

"I need you guys to dust the house, and in particular, this window ledge. Also, I need a casting of a set of footprints."

The tech followed Jason to where the detective had seen the shoe prints. Jason pointed at them.

The tech nodded. "Yes, sir."

Looking from the back door, the

small yard behind the duplex opened onto an alley. Jason and Nina walked back to where they could see for two blocks in either direction. The alley eventually hit a street at both ends.

Nina summed it up.

"This might explain why no one heard or saw anything. Easy to come and go without being noticed."

Jason was nodding.

"Almost perfect cover."

They walked back to the front of the house. Nina grabbed the file out of the car.

"The address for the ex-wife is in here. Do you want to go talk to her?"

"Yeah, we're done here."

Chapter 6

Chelsea Morris took a quick look at the clock. Fifteen minutes more, and her shift was over. She grabbed the coffee pot for the hundredth time today, and went over to Mr. Perkins. Ever since Chelsea started at Daylight Donuts, the elderly man had sat in her station. In all that time, he'd never ordered food. Just coffee, black and hot, a half-cup at a time.

"Here you go, Mr. Perkins."

"Just a half-cup."

Chelsea smiled, and obediently stopped at the halfway point in his cup. They played out this dance all the time.

"You want a donut?"

"No thank you, young lady. I think I'll just have coffee today."

Mr. Perkins had lost his wife ten years ago. He had told Chelsea about his beloved Dolly many times, and Chelsea always listened patiently. She didn't know how old Mr. Perkins was, but she guessed him in his seventies.

Talking to people of his generation was easy for Chelsea. As the last of seven kids, her parents were already in their late forties when she came along.

Sitting next to Mr. Perkins was a young man drinking a mocha latte. He hadn't said two words except to order. He got up with his coffee and headed for the door. Sitting under the saltshaker was a twenty-dollar bill.

Chelsea picked up the tip and called after the man.

"Thank you!"

He turned, smiled at her, and left without a word.

She turned back to Mr. Perkins.

"Mr. Perkins, my shift is getting ready to end. I'll see you on Wednesday."

"Very well. I was just thinking of leaving myself."

Chelsea smiled at him, patted his hand, and went into the back room. Her friend Trudi was just coming in.

"Hey, Trudi. How ya doin'?"

"Good. How's my BFF?"

"I'm off for two days, which means I am awesome!"

"Don't rub it in."

Chelsea punched out, heading

directly out the door before her boss could ask her to do any last-minute chores. She'd just finished her sixth straight day, and her feet were killing her.

She went out the back door and walked across the gravel parking lot toward her Chevy Cavalier. It was red, *was* being the key word, but now carried an aged, rusty brown color over most of its body. It never left her stranded, so she hung on to it.

She threw her apron across the front seat and climbed in. The familiar scent of coconut from the tiny surfboard hanging from her mirror filled her senses. After a traumatic event in her teen years, She'd spent some time in California. Her parents had sent her to live with an aunt in Long Beach.

It was there she'd caught the surfing bug, as well as got married. Neither lasted very long. Still, it was an exciting time, and the smell of coconut reminded her of those days.

She pulled her seat belt across her tiny shoulders and snagged some of her jet-black hair. At just five-foot, everything seemed just a little too big, including her seat belt, which didn't fit comfortably. She untangled her hair and snapped the belt.

Something moved in her rear-view mirror, and before she could react, a gun pushed against the back of her head.

"Start the car."

She started to cry, but did as she was told.

"Now drive."

"Where?"

"Turn right out of the lot, and go north."

"Why? What do you want from me?"

"No questions; just drive."

She drove until they got to Huebner road.

"Turn right."

Chelsea did, and after less than a mile, he instructed her to turn left into a cement plant. The construction yard was huge, and she didn't see anyone around. After directing her to the back corner of the lot, the man had her pull up alongside an old van.

"Stop here."

The gun had left her head while they drove, but Chelsea could feel it pushing into her back through the seat. Now it returned to her head.

"Get out."

Chelsea slid out of the front seat at the same time the man got out of the back, the gun trained on her constantly.

"Put your hands behind your back."

"Please don't hurt me. I don't have much money, just today's tips, but you can have them."

She had stopped crying, but her voice still trembled.

"I said put your hands behind you!"

She did, and felt handcuffs click onto both wrists, quickly followed by a hood being pulled over her head. Panic filled her, and she started to cry again. Her captor steered her forward until she heard what sounded like a sliding door open.

"Get in and lie down."

Chelsea fell forward onto some carpet that smelled of oil and grease. She rolled on her side in an effort to be more comfortable, and to try to look out from under the hood. She couldn't see a thing, and when he slid the door shut she felt cut off from civilization. Isolated in a world filled with fear.

She heard a door open and close.

"Don't move, don't say a word. I won't hesitate to kill you if you aren't doing exactly what I tell you."

Chelsea lay on her side as the van started and they began to move. She began to pray quietly in between her sobs.

****

Ed Garland's ex-wife lived on the opposite side of the city, and it took the two detectives almost an hour to get there.

Rita Garland's address was a second-floor apartment on a quiet street in East San Antonio. She opened the door, but didn't invite the detectives in.

Tall, skinny, with bleach blonde hair, and a down-turned mouth that gave her a seemingly permanent frown. Jason tried to see into the apartment while he talked.

"Mrs. Garland?"

"Yes."

"My name is Detective Strong, and this is Detective Jefferson. We're here about your husband."

"My husband and I are divorced. I'm not sure how I can help."

"You told the officer you weren't surprised to learn your ex-husband is missing. Can I ask why?"

She seemed unsure how to answer. Finally, she pushed the door open all the way.

"You might as well come in. No

sense in you standing out in the heat."

The two detectives followed Rita Garland into the small living room, and, as Nina shut the door behind them, the room went dark. After letting their eyes adjust, Jason took a seat on the couch while Nina stayed standing by the door. She had her notepad out.

Opposite Jason was a recliner, which Rita Garland settled into with grunt. A half-empty glass of caramel-colored liquid sat on the side table. Jason figured scotch.

She noticed his stare. "Would you like a drink?"

Both Jason and Nina shook their heads.

"No, thank you."

Rita took a sip of her drink and looked at Jason over the top of her glass.

"Detective…Strong, did you say?"

"Yes, ma'am."

"My ex-husband is a troubled man. A fact I wasn't aware of when we got married."

"Troubled how?"

"Emotionally, mentally. Not crazy or anything like that. It just always seemed that something at the edges of his consciousness tempered his enjoyment of life. Depressed, I guess."

"Is he on anti-depressants?"

"Not that I'm aware of. He's how he is because of something that happened before I met him."

"Did he say what?"

"His best friend committed suicide. Ed never told me the whole story, but he did tell me he was there when it happened, and he felt responsible."

"Why?"

"Don't know. I guess Ed thought he should have stopped him, but he never told me for sure."

"Do you know when this happened?"

Rita shook her head.

"Just that Ed was a teenager. About ten or twelve years ago, I figure."

Nina spoke up.

"Do you know how the friend died?"

"Shot himself."

"And you mentioned you didn't know before your marriage, are you suggesting the friend's suicide was responsible for your divorce?"

"Oh, I'm not suggesting, I'm sayin.' Look, there's a lot of things that go into a failed marriage, but that particular cloud never seemed to lift. It was like he felt he didn't deserve anything good to happen to him."

"Do you have any idea where he might have gone?"

"Not a clue. Like I said, we don't talk much, but he's always been a homebody. I can't imagine anywhere he would want to take off to."

Her words were becoming more slurred, and the glass was empty. The two detectives got up to leave.

"Mrs. Garland, thank you for your time. We won't trouble you any longer."

Rita Garland got up as well, but not to see them to the door. She walked over to a cabinet and took out a bottle. She poured a refill as Nina and Jason let themselves out.

Chapter 7

Donnie stopped behind the house and turned off the van. Getting out and sliding the side door open, he forced Chelsea out and onto her feet.

She had stopped sobbing on the way to the farm, and Donnie was relieved—he never liked hearing girls cry. He steered her up the back steps and into the house.

"Where are we? Where are you taking me?"

"Where we are isn't important."

Donnie opened the door to the basement and removed the hood. He watched as she blinked repeatedly, trying adjust to the light.

"We're going down some steps. Just take your time, and I won't let you fall."

Her hands still cuffed behind her, the girl didn't speak as she focused on taking one step at a time. Donnie held the gun to her back. When they made it to the bottom, he motioned toward the open door of the second cell and watched as the girl's eyes grew wide with horror.

****

Chelsea tried to keep it together. It was all so unreal, being taken, walked down into this man's basement, and now he was motioning her toward a small door.

When she didn't move, he pushed her from behind with the butt of the gun, and she stumbled into a small room. Her eyes caught sight of a blanket on the floor, chain coiled on it. Her blood ran cold, and she spun around to face her captor, trying to get back out of the cell.

"Please don't do this! Please let me go."

He blocked her way.

"Sit down on the blanket."

"No, please no."

"NOW!"

She collapsed onto the blanket. Her captor took the chain and wrapped it tightly around her leg twice. He ran a padlock through the end link and the one of links leading to the wall. It snapped shut, and after testing it, he took her cuffs off.

Chelsea rubbed her wrists and tried not to cry as the door shut. She heard another padlock snap shut, followed by footsteps going upstairs. Everything went quiet.

Chelsea had to let her eyes adjust again, this time to darkness, and realized she could hear breathing. "Hello? Is someone there?"

"Hi."

The voice startled her. She hadn't even considered someone else might be down here, and her heart pounded. She wasn't alone.

"Who are you?"

"My name is Ed. You?"

"Chelsea."

A brief moment of silence hung in the air before he spoke again.

"What's your last name?"

"Morris."

"Oh."

Chelsea scooted as close as she could manage to the wall where the voice came from.

"How long have you been here?"

"Two days, I think."

"Why are we here? Do you know?"

"I asked him. He just said I would know soon enough."

Chelsea heard the man scoot closer to the wall, his chain dragging on the floor, before he spoke.

"Do you know who he is?"

"Not a clue. I don't remember ever seeing him before. Do you?"

The man on the other side of the wall sounded tired.

"No. I don't know him, either."

Quiet returned to the room. She scooted back to her blanket and tried to look for a weakness in the walls of the room. Everything looked solid. She tested the chain. She wasn't going anywhere.

She resumed the praying she had started in the van.

****

Trudi had an uneasy feeling. It wasn't like Chelsea to be late, and her friend hadn't answered her calls in two days.

Sitting at the counter was Mr. Perkins. He had asked, about every ten minutes, when Chelsea would be in.

"Miss Trudi, have you heard from Miss Chelsea?"

"Not yet, Mr. Perkins. I'm sure

she'll be along any time now. Do you need a refill?"

"Please, just a half-cup."

Trudi knew the drill just as well as Chelsea, but for Mr. Perkins, only his favorite really made him happy. And truth was she wasn't sure her friend would be along any minute. Something wasn't right. She tried calling again.

"This is Chelsea; you know what to do…"

Trudi hung up. Her shift ended in a half-hour, and she had decided to go over to her friend's house if Chelsea hadn't shown up by then.

Mr. Chambers came out of the back office and signaled Trudi over. "Where's Chelsea? She's over an hour late."

"I don't know, Boss. I'm going over to her house after work. I'll call and let you know what I find."

"A 'No call, No show' is supposed to be instant termination. I don't want to do that to one of my best girls. She better have a good reason."

"I'm sure she does. I'll have her call you when I get over there. I'm going right after my shift."

****

Trudi got to her friend's house around noon. Chelsea's car wasn't there, and mail was sticking out of the mailbox.

She parked on the driveway, and entered through the side door to the garage. When she got to the utility room door, she found it locked.

Chelsea had shown her where she kept the spare key, and she opened the door to find the house dark. Something felt very wrong.

"Chelsea!"

No answer, no sound at all. Mugsy, Chelsea's cat, came around the corner.

"Hi, Mugsy." She reached down and scratched him on the head. "Chelsea!"

She stuck her head in the door, looking toward the kitchen. Nothing. She walked through the entire house. The litter box in the kitchen was full and hadn't been cleaned in days. The cat's water was empty.

"Chelsea!"

Convinced her friend wasn't there, she took out her phone and dialed 911.

****

Jason and Nina had started first thing in the morning on the task of finding out everything they could about Ed Garland. They went to where he worked, and to the golf club where he was to meet Jerry Baker. No one had seen the missing man.

Nina had managed to get a check on his debit and credit card activity. Neither had been used in three days.

They arrived back at the station around three-thirty in the afternoon. Jason had one stop he wanted to make before briefing Lieutenant Banks.

"I'm going to see Doc Josie."

Nina didn't want to face Sarah Banks alone.

"Mind if I tag along?"

"Fine with me."

They took the stairs down to the basement and went through the double glass doors leading into the forensic department.

Affectionately called 'Doc Josie,' Dr. Jocelyn Carter was the head of the Forensic Science Department. Short with curly, brown hair and black, wire-framed glasses around blue eyes, she looked like the classic college professor. Some might describe her as 'frumpy,' but she's brilliant. The detectives found her sitting at her desk.

"Josie. How we doin'?"

"Jason. What a nice surprise."

"You've met Nina Jefferson?"

"Yes, of course. Hi, Nina."

Nina gave the doc a smile as Jason sat down in one of the two chairs facing Doc Josie's desk.

"So Doc, what did your crew find at the Garland house?"

"Not much. We found prints on the ledge and a doorknob, neither of which belonged to Mr. Garland. We ran them through the AFIS fingerprint system, but no luck. Evidently, the person who left the prints doesn't have a record."

Jason had figured the fingerprint database would be useless. He knew most people who didn't conceal their prints did so because they knew there was no record of them.

"What about the shoe print?"

"Size nine running shoe. Nike, but not rare enough to be much help except as a match to the correct shoe."

"Okay. Well, not much to go on. Thanks."

"No problem. Always glad to see you."

****

Jason and Nina found Lieutenant

Banks sitting in her office. Nina rapped on the doorframe before entering. The lieutenant glanced up, before her eyes turned back to her paperwork. "What's up?"

Nina stayed by the door, and Jason had to slip past her to speak to the lieutenant. He gave Nina a knowing smile.

Afraid to go into the lion's den, huh?

Jason pulled up a chair. "Just wanted to give you an update on the Garland case."

"Okay, shoot."

He informed her they had subpoenaed Garland's phone records, and shared the news from Doc Josie. When he was done, she looked up from her paperwork and crossed her arms.

"Not much. Any ideas besides the phone records?"

Before Jason could answer, the phone rang. The lieutenant pushed the speaker button.

"Banks."

"Lieutenant, this is Doc Josie."

"Yeah, Doc. What's up?"

"The car we recovered this afternoon from the missing Morris woman, it's got prints that don't belong to her."

"Got an ID?"

"Sort of."

"Can you be more specific, Doctor?"

"Sure. By the way, do you know where Detective Strong is?"

"As a matter of fact, I do. He's sitting here, listening to our conversation."

"Oh. Hey, Jason."

Jason let out a small laugh.

"Hi, Doc."

Doc Josie continued.

"Well, to answer the question about ID on the prints, I don't have a name, but I do have a match. It's the same ones we pulled from Ed Garland's duplex."

Lieutenant Banks sat up, grabbed a file on her desk, and slid it across to Jason.

"I just passed the file to Strong. Did you find anything else in the car?"

"Not so far."

"Okay, Doc. Thanks for the update. I'm assigning the Morris case to Strong and Jefferson, so keep them in the loop."

The lieutenant hit the disconnect button without waiting for a reply.

"Alright, you two better review the Morris file and see if it gives you any direction on Garland."

Jason got up and headed for the door.

"Yes, ma'am."

It seemed they would be working the missing persons cases awhile longer.

Chapter 8

Big thunderclouds to the west darkened the sky, a spitting rain just starting, as Donnie parked and got out. He was now halfway through the first phase of Billy's plan, and he wanted to keep his brother up to speed on how they were doing.

"Hi, Billy. Good news, we're halfway. Chelsea is in her cell."

Donnie listened intently before starting to pace back and forth in front of the grave.

"Billy, I'm doing this as fast as I can. It's not easy, and you're not here to help." Donnie stopped moving and stared down at his brother. "I gotta go. I'll be back when I have more news."

Donnie turned and walked off. The rain picked up when he got in the van, and he sat looking out the window as a full downpour began.

Hurry up, he says. He doesn't seem

*to appreciate what I've accomplished.
Haven't I done everything he's asked?
I've had to do all the work, and I've done
a good job. He doesn't seem to
understand how hard all of this is!*

Donnie started the van and turned on the wipers. The weather it seemed was in the same bad mood he was.

****

Jason sat at his desk going over the file they received from Lieutenant Banks.

Chelsea Morris, previously Chelsea Burt, was a waitress at Daylight Donuts in the center of the city. She lived in a house owned by her parents, and had returned to San Antonio from California several years ago.

Jason looked out the window at the rain. Summer rain was rare, and the downpour was a welcome sight. Nina was checking the missing girl's name for priors.

"No record. Drivers license clean except for a speeding ticket several years ago."

"Okay. The file says Miss Morris was reported missing by a friend at work. We need to go see her."

"I'm putting in a request for

Morris's phone records. That will give us two sets to compare. We should have them in the morning."

Lieutenant Patton got off the elevator and stopped at Jason's desk on the way to his office. "How's it going with the missing person case?"

Jason leaned back in his chair and looked up at the lieutenant. "It's now a two-missing-persons case."

"Really? More than one?"

"Yeah. Two cases connected by a set of prints. We may be a while getting free from the clutches of Lieutenant Banks."

John Patton smiled.

"You make it sound like she's a spider who has you in her web."

Nina snorted.

"That's an excellent description."

The lieutenant looked at Nina and back at Jason.

"Don't be fooled. She's very good, kind of abrupt I know, but good."

"Yes, sir."

The two detectives exchanged glances as Lieutenant Patton went to his office.

Jason had noticed some admiration in the voice of his boss. "Apparently, he's familiar with her. I think he's impressed by her."

Nina laughed. "Yeah, or afraid of her!"

It was Jason's turn to laugh, but he knew better. John Patton wasn't afraid of anybody.

****

Chelsea Morris sat on the blanket in her cell listening to the rain. She still hadn't been able to sleep, but she was getting hungry. She heard footsteps coming down the stairs and her heart started to pound.

"Were those footsteps?"

It was Ed. He hadn't said anything in hours.

"Yes."

The steps got closer until her captor's face peered through the bars. He unlocked her door, came in, and set a tray down on the floor. Chelsea was trying to be strong, to not give this man any satisfaction by keeping her, but she couldn't stop herself from pleading.

"Please…please let me go. I won't say anything. I don't even know where we are."

"Sorry. Can't."

"Why? Why can't you?"

"Look, just shut up and eat your food!"

He left the cell and locked it. Chelsea started to cry again, and lunged toward the door, but her chain stopped her. She spotted the food and hunger took over. She devoured the bar and drank the shake in one gulp.

The man gave food to Ed before returning upstairs, the eerie silence falling over her again. She curled up on her blanket, making herself as small as possible. She wanted to disappear.

****

Donnie closed the door at the top of the basement steps. Pulling out a kitchen chair, he sat at the table and laid his head in his hands. It had not been a good day.

He'd been rude to the girl downstairs, something his momma wouldn't tolerate, and become angry with Billy. He knew the fight with Billy was causing him to be so unhappy.

I'll focus on getting Suzanne; that'll patch things up with Billy. When I have her, I'll go tell him I'm sorry and give him the good news. He'll be much happier once I have his girlfriend in a cell

.He fell asleep at the kitchen table.

Chapter 9

The next morning, Devin James was waiting for Jason in the parking lot of the police station. A crime reporter for the San Antonio News, he was quickly becoming a thorn in Jason's side.

Black, six-foot-three, balding, with a big smile that hid a cynical mind, he had a way of asking the questions Jason didn't want to answer.

"Morning, JD."

"What did I tell you about calling me that?"

The reporter ignored the rebuke.

"Word on the street has you investigating missing persons. Not your usual gig. Any truth to that?"

Jason didn't like being ambushed, especially first thing in the morning. On top of that, it annoyed him how James managed to get info he shouldn't have.

"You know I can't comment about ongoing investigations."

Jason noticed the reporter seemed to be looking past him, ignoring his response. When Jason turned to see what caught James's eye, he saw Nina coming across the lot from her car. He gave her a wave. "Watch out. You're being stalked!"

Nina laughed. "I don't see any predators around here."

"Actually, it's a *reporterus ignoramus*. Pretty tame, really."

James feigned injury by clutching at his chest. "Detective Strong! You cut me and I bleed."

Smiling, he took Nina's hand.

"I don't believe we've met. Jason, who is this angel?"

"That's Nina Jefferson. Nina, this is Devin James. I believe I mentioned him."

Devin practically purred. "Enchanted."

Jason chuckled. "That 'angel' you refer to, Devin, might just break your arm if you get out of line."

It was Nina's turn to smile. "Excuse me, Mr. James. We have work to do."

With that, she unwound herself from the reporter's grip and joined Jason walking toward the station doors.

Once inside, they went by Lieutenant Banks' office, but she wasn't in yet. Jason suggested they go see Chelsea Morris's friend at Daylight Donuts. Nina agreed.

When they returned to the parking lot, Devin was gone. Nina grabbed the file out of her car, and they left for the north side of the city.

****

Suzanne Cooper was having a good day. Her chair at 'TINA'S HAIR SALON' had stayed busy since early morning. The tall woman with auburn hair was popular with her clients, and today they had tipped her especially well.

"Mrs. Harkin, can I get you to move over to the hair dryers."

"Of course, dear."

Suzanne carried the bunched-up smock around the elderly woman, as they made their way to the dryer chair. When Mrs. Harkin was settled into place, Suzanne lowered the helmet over her head, and set the timer for fifteen minutes. "I'll be back to get you in a bit."

Mrs. Harkin smiled at her and opened a People magazine.

As Suzanne walked back to her chair, she saw a young man get out of a gray Subaru, come in, and stop at the desk. She didn't recognize him. "Can I help you?"

He was average height and build, with black hair that didn't look like it needed to be cut.

"Yes, I need a haircut. Do you have an opening?"

"Let me see who's not busy."

"No. I want *you* to cut my hair."

"Oh. Well, I have about fifteen minutes. I guess I can squeeze you in."

"Great!"

He smiled at her, and Suzanne felt there was something vaguely familiar about him. He came around the desk, and she wrapped a smock around him as he settled into her chair. "Do I know you?"

"No. A friend of mine, Chelsea Morris, said you were the best."

Suzanne couldn't place the name, but she had people walk in and get haircuts all the time.

"I guess I don't remember the name. You don't look like you need much of a haircut. What did you want done?"

"Oh, just thin it some, trim the sideburns, and tidy up the neckline. I hate when things aren't tidy."

Suzanne couldn't help but chuckle. "Okay...tidy up, it is. What's your name?"

"Donnie."

"Nice to meet you, Donnie."

Within ten minutes she was done, and he examined himself in the mirror.

"Do you have a straight razor?"

"I don't, but Silvia does. Why?"

"I like to get the thin hair below the sideburns."

"Okay. Sit tight. I'll borrow hers."

She went two stations down and returned with the blade. She ran it below his sideburns, brushed off the clippings, and removed the smock as he stood up.

"How much?"

"Twelve dollars."

He gave her two twenties.

"Keep it."

"Thanks! That's very generous."

"It's my pleasure. After all, you squeezed me in."

He smiled, turned, and left.

Suzanne just stared after him.

That was odd. I need to look in my address book for a Chelsea Morris.

The timer went off, and she went to get Mrs. Harkin, putting the stranger out of her thoughts.

****

The detectives parked out front of Daylight Donuts, and a waitress with Trudi on her nametag met them at the door.

"Two?"

Jason smiled at the small redhead. She had green eyes and a bright smile.

"Are you Trudi Fulton?"

Her smile disappeared.

"Yes."

"My name is Detective Strong and this is my partner, Detective Jefferson."

He showed her his ID.

"Is this about Chelsea?"

"Yes. Do you have time for a few questions?"

"Sure. Let me tell Gloria."

She crossed to the back of the restaurant, spoke to the other waitress, and returned. Guiding them to a table near the door, she sat across from the two detectives.

Jason looked into her eyes. He sensed fear lingering, and knew it would probably be there for a while.

"You doing okay, Trudi?"

"I'm making it. Work both helps and hurts. I'm glad to be busy, but then it's hard when someone like Mr. Perkins comes in."

"Mr. Perkins?"

"He's an elderly widower who doesn't like anyone but Chelsea to wait on him. He's taking it hard."

"Is there anyone else who seemed overly interested in Chelsea? Maybe pestered her or she mentioned she was afraid of?"

"Nobody. She seemed happy and worry free."

"The last time you saw her was when she clocked out the other day?"

"Yeah. We worked opposite shifts, and I was just coming in."

Nina, who was taking notes, looked up.

"Where do you park?"

"In back. There's a gravel lot for employees."

"And you didn't notice anything unusual that day?"

"No. Well, now that I think about it, there was one thing."

"Oh?"

"When I got here, there was a guy sitting on the grass behind the lot, drinking a coffee. I didn't think anything of it at the time."

Jason touched her hand.

"I know this is hard, but I need you to focus on that moment in time. Try to recall anything about him."

"I only glanced at him. He was sitting down so I don't really know how tall he was," She closed her eyes as she concentrated. "Let's see. He was white, short hair, I don't remember a beard. Jeans and a yellow shirt."

"Had you ever seen him before?"

"I don't think so."

"Was there anyone else here that day?"

"Just the manager, Mr. Chambers."

"Is he here now?"

"Yeah, in back. I'll get him."

The interview with Mr. Chambers didn't produce any new clues. Jason asked Trudi to take them to the spot where she'd seen the man sitting. She walked them through the small kitchen and out the back door of the donut shop.

They stepped out onto a gravel parking lot. It backed up to some woods and only had one driveway to the street. It made a good place for an ambush.

Nina favored the theory.

"I bet he was waiting in or near her car."

They did a search around the spot where the man had been, but didn't find anything useful. Jason realized Nina was probably right.

"Where was Miss Morris's car

found?"

Nina looked in the file.

"About two miles from here, a cement plant."

"And to get there, what direction?"

"She'd leave and turn right toward Huebner Road."

Jason turned to Trudi.

"Which direction would Chelsea normally turn to go home?"

Trudi thought for a minute.

"Left. She takes the Beltway north."

"Thanks for your help, Trudi. We'll be in touch when we have news."

Jason headed for the car with Nina trying to catch up.

"Jason, where's the fire?"

"Traffic camera headquarters."

Nina smiled.

"Of course. We can probably track her movements!"

"Let's hope so. If we can spot her car, we can find out if you're right about her being ambushed here."

Chapter 10

Suzanne pulled her teal-colored Ford Focus into the Quikstop. Her gas light was on, and a cold drink seemed to be in order. It'd been a busy day, and she was worn out. She filled her car and went into the store.

Something with a lot of caffeine is called for if I'm ever going to get any housework done tonight.

Grabbing a Red Bull, she went to the counter. While the guy if front of her paid, she got out her debit card, and noticed her address book was missing from its usual pocket. She rummaged around, looking for it.

Where is that stupid thing! I hate this purse; it's like a bottomless pit.

The man in front was done, so she stepped up. While the clerk ran her card, she continued to search for the address book.

"Thank you, ma'am."

She reclaimed her card, picked up her drink, and went to the car.

Maybe it's at home. It had better be; all my clients are in that book.

****

Donnie sat in his car across from the Quikstop gas station. Resting next to him on the seat, an address book decorated with pink flowers. He watched as Suzanne Cooper got gas, went inside, and then searched her bag for something while standing in line.

It's not in there, Miss Cooper. I'll bring it to you later.

He smiled to himself. After he got Suzanne Cooper, there would be just one more.

****

Jason got on State Highway 281 going southeast; the fifteen-minute drive would bring them to the I-410 access road and their destination, the Texas Department of Transportation.

Nina had brought with her the phone records of Ed Garland and Chelsea Morris. She was nearly three-quarters of the way through them, and still hadn't found a connection. She wasn't giving up, even though it was tedious work.

"Bingo!"

"What?"

"I've got a phone number from Ed Garland's record that also shows up on the records of Chelsea Morris."

"Whose is it?"

"That's odd. It's McCollum High School."

"Really? Why's that odd?"

"That's the school I went to."

Jason laughed. "Not so weird, a lot of people went to that school. Were they incoming or outgoing calls?"

"Incoming. The school called them."

"We'll need to go by. Maybe we can find out who made the calls."

Jason turned into the parking lot of the DOT office and parked. "At least we have a connection besides just the finger prints."

****

Suzanne arrived home a few minutes after getting gas. Home was a white, single-story bungalow with a shake-shingle roof and tan shutters.

She'd never married, and her only

companion was a Yorkie named Tizzy. The name had come from the way the dog greeted Chelsea at the end of the day.

Suzanne let herself in, and the dog met her at the door. They went through the standard 'pick me up and give kisses' before she put Tizzy out in the backyard to do her business.

She went looking for her address book. After several minutes of searching, she found herself standing in the kitchen.

Where is that stupid book? My purse sits by my station all day, and I don't remember taking the book out once.

She decided to wait until she checked work tomorrow before going into a full-blown panic. In the meantime, the Red Bull was kicking in, and there was laundry to do.

****

Jason and Nina came through the double glass doors into the cool reception hall of the Texas DOT offices.

"Can I help you?"

Jason showed his badge to the twenty-something blonde at the desk.

"I'm Detective Strong, this is Detective Jefferson. We need to speak with Jack Burns."

The girl immediately looked concerned, and picked up the phone without saying anything. "Mr. Burns, there's two detectives here to see you."

She listened for a minute before hanging up. "He'll be right out."

"Thanks."

Jason called Lieutenant Patton on the way over to find out if he knew someone, and Jack Burns was the name the lieutenant had given him. The lieutenant had said he and Burns went way back.

A short and thin, but well tanned, man with silver hair came through the glass door at the far end of the reception area. Jason guessed he didn't spend all his time in an office.

"Jack Burns?"

"Yes, that's me. How can I help you?"

"My name is Detective Strong, this is Detective Jefferson. Is there somewhere we can talk?"

"Sure, let's go to my office."

As they walked, the DOT official looked from Jason to Nina. "Did I do something?"

Nina gave him a reassuring smile.

"No, sir. We're involved in an investigation, and we believe you may be able to help."

"Oh. In here."

He led them through the glass door and then directed them immediately to their right, into a spacious office.

Jason and Nina both took the chairs offered them. Jack Burns shut the door before going around his desk and sitting down. "Alright, Detectives. How can I help?"

Jason produced a sheet of paper; a map with Daylight Donuts and the location where Chelsea Morris's car was found.

"We need to see if you have any cameras along this route."

He handed the paper to Burns, and after examining it for a minute, the DOT official punched some numbers into the computer on his desk. When he was done, he turned the computer monitor toward the two detectives.

"I have one camera on this route. It's at Huebner."

Jason couldn't make sense of the multiple cameras being displayed.

"Which one is that?"

Burns clicked a couple more keys, and the screen changed to just one image. Jason stared intently.

"Can you call up specific times for

these cameras?"

"Sure, but they're not movie cameras. These are still shots that refresh about every five minutes."

Jason handed the DOT official another piece of paper. "This is the time and date we need."

Burns started pushing more keys, and spun a roller ball on his mouse, until he came to a specific frame on the cameras. "Okay, what are we looking for?"

Jason took a quick glance at his notes. "Nineteen-ninety-five Chevy Cavalier."

Burns started clicking a button, and with each click, a new image showed. Nina saw it first.

"There!"

Jason agreed that had to be the car. "That's it. Can you blow it up?"

"Some, but I'm limited."

The picture zoomed in. The vehicle was driving away, and was at least a hundred feet past the camera when the shot was taken.

They couldn't see Chelsea, but there was a clear image of a man in the back seat. Nina said what both detectives were thinking.

"She was stalked. He was waiting

outside and ambushed her before the drive home."

Jason just stared at the image. This confirmed his suspicions that both their missing persons were likely chosen and hunted. But more importantly, they didn't know if this man had more targets.

He stood and shook hands with Jack Burns.

"Can you print me a copy of the photo?"

"Sure." Jack punched some more keys. "Be back in a minute."

When Burns left the office, Jason turned to Nina.

"The best connection we have between the victims is the phone number from the high school. We need to go there next."

The DOT official returned with the photo, and the detectives headed for their car.

Chapter 11

Suzanne finished folding the load of towels and went to the kitchen. The Red Bull was wearing off, and she decided it was time to relax with some TV. She got some ice from the fridge, poured herself a Diet Pepsi, and just as she was about to sit down, the doorbell rang.

Tizzy raced to the door and started her incessant barking, which announced every visitor's arrival.

"Tizzy! Shush! Tizzy!"

Suzanne opened the door to find her walk-in customer from earlier standing there. She raised her eyebrows in surprise.

"Oh, hi. Can I help you?"

"Hi. I don't know if you remember me, but I was in your shop today."

"Of course. Donnie, isn't it? Is there something wrong?"

"Well, in an odd coincidence, I stopped at the Quikstop a while ago and..."

Tizzy was going nuts, barking and baring her teeth at the stranger.

"Tizzy, shush. That's enough!"

"...Anyway, I found your address book lying next to the gas pumps. I live just around the corner, so I thought I'd bring it to you."

"Oh, that's wonderful. I was looking all over for it."

Tizzy kept at it, barking, and threatening to charge the man, despite her tiny size.

"Tizzy! Excuse me while I lock her in the bedroom."

Suzanne scooped up the dog, walked to the bedroom, put the dog in the room, and shut the door. When she turned around, the man was standing in the middle of the living room, a gun pointed at her.

"Don't scream, or I'll shoot you where you stand."

****

Jason and Nina took I-35 south to Military Trail, over to Commercial Ave, and then south to Formosa. Even though Jason knew where the school was, Nina was giving him directions.

"Okay, the school's just a block that way."

"Detective, I think you're kinda excited to be going back to your old school."

Nina saw she was exposed and laughed.

"Yeah, I guess. My years at McCollum High were good ones. And unlike like you, my high school years weren't two decades ago!"

"Ouch! You're brutal."

They stopped in front of the office and got out. Nina scanned the collection of buildings. "Hasn't changed much."

"Lead the way, ex-alum."

They walked up the sidewalk to a set of double doors and found them un-locked. School was out for the summer, so basic staff and maintenance would be the only people there.

They came in out of the heat, and Jason removed his sunglasses. The office was immediately on the right, and through a large glass window, they could see a collection of desks. No one appeared to be there, so Jason stuck his head through the office door.

"Hello?"

From a somewhere in the back, they heard a woman's voice.

"Be right there!"

While they waited, Nina watched as Jason scanned the photos on the wall.

"Looking for something?"

"Yeah. Thought they might have your detention records framed."

"Hey! I was a good girl."

Jason rolled his eyes and laughed.

A woman dressed in gray slacks came into the room. "May I help you?"

She wore a black, button-down blouse, and black, patent leather shoes. With short, brown hair and hazel eyes, she carried herself with an official bearing. Jason guessed her to be in her early fifties.

"I hope so. My name is Detective Strong, and this is my partner Detective Jefferson. We're with SAPD."

They both showed their badges.

"I'm Janice Hayes, the principal's secretary. Is there a problem?"

"No. We're involved in an investigation, and the number of McCollum High has showed up on a couple phone records. The calls were outgoing from here. We'd like to find out who made the calls and why they were made."

"Do you have the numbers called?"

Nina took the phone records out of

a manila folder she was carrying and handed them to the secretary. "I've highlighted them."

Janice Hayes followed the highlighted numbers with her finger, across to the names. "I made both calls, Chelsea Morris and Ed Garland were on my list."

Nina took the reports back and put them in the folder. "Your list?"

"Yes. I'm helping with notifications of the ten-year class reunion coming up. The class president gave me some of the names. I told her I had some extra time and I'd be glad to help."

"May we see the list?"

"Sure. I'll be right back."

Janice Hayes returned in less than a minute with two sheets of paper.

"I have about fifty names to call. We use email for most of the notifications, but these are the ones we only have phone numbers for."

Jason took one sheet and Nina the other. Jason found one of the names immediately. "Ed Garland, fifth name down on this sheet."

Nina's sheet had the other. "Chelsea Morris, near the bottom."

Jason gave his sheet back to the secretary. "Can we get a copy of these?"

The secretary took Nina's, as well. "Sure. Give me a couple minutes."

When she was gone, Jason started thinking aloud.

"Okay. Both victims received calls about the reunion, along with about fifty others on these lists. In addition, there's the list the class president is calling. Assuming it's roughly the same size, that's somewhere around a hundred names."

"That's just the call list. There's apparently an email list also."

Jason nodded.

"I'm thinking we start with the call list. Nothing has showed on the email list that we know of. Until there's a connection to that list, we need to limit our search as much as possible."

"So, you think the connection between victims is the reunion?"

"It's about all we've got for right now."

Nina was skeptical. "Okay, following that logic, our killer's name should also be on these lists."

"Maybe, but not necessarily. If he's targeting this group, or some of the group, it might be because he's *not* on the list. When we get back, we need to run a record check on all the names on this list."

Janice Hayes returned with four pages. "I copied both my list and the class president's."

She handed them to Nina, who put them in the folder. "Who is the class president, anyway?"

"Cindy Butler. Her name's at the top of each sheet, along with her phone number."

"And when is the reunion?" Nina asked.

"The fifth of next month, here in the gym."

"Thank you. We'll be in touch if we need anything else."

The secretary looked at Jason. "Can I ask why Ed Garland and Chelsea Morris are of particular interest?"

"They're missing."

"Missing? Both of them?"

"Yes, ma'am. Both of them."

Chapter 12

Donnie turned the corner and pulled in behind the small strip plaza. Cuffed in the backseat of her own car was Suzanne Cooper. The van was waiting for him, and he transferred his captive to it, putting a hood over her head once she was inside.

The plaza sat about a mile from Suzanne's house, and Donnie had walked to get her. He would leave her car here and take her to the farm.

Donnie put the hoods over his captives' heads to protect the location of his home. He didn't want them to know where they'd been, *if* they survived.

He started the van and drove out from behind the plaza. Twenty minutes and he'd be home with only one remaining task in the first phase.

****

Suzanne lay as still as she could. She was trying to trace in her mind where they were going. She knew they'd gone to the plaza near her house, but after only a few minutes, she realized it was hopeless. She didn't even know what direction they were headed.

She struggled to grasp what was happening. Time had ceased to exist, and her mind reeled with possibilities of what waited when the van stopped. She wanted out of the hood and the darkness it brought, but she was terrified of what she might see at the end of their trip.

She didn't know how long they had been driving, but she felt the van slow and make a hard turn onto a gravel road. She could hear the dirt and rock kicking up beneath her. After just a moment or two, the van ceased moving and the engine sputtered to silence.

She heard the driver's door open, then the van's side door slid open. Her captor grabbed her by the feet to drag her out, but she kicked wildly. He let go. Next to her ear came the distinct sound of a gun being cocked.

Click!

Her heart stopped. "No, no. I'm sorry. I'll get out."

Again, she felt the tug on her feet,

but this time she didn't resist. When her knees were past the edge of the door, he took her by the shoulders, and stood her up.

"Walk slowly, I'll guide you. Don't do anything stupid, and you won't be hurt."

It took all the strength she could muster just to nod her head once.

They walked a short distance and then up a couple steps. She heard a door open and sensed they had moved indoors. The hood came off.

She blinked at the brightness, trying to focus, and found the man staring at her.

"Please don't hurt me. What did I do? Why are you doing this?"

He ignored her and pointed the gun toward the basement steps. She didn't move. Again, he pulled the hammer back on the gun.

She willed herself to move slowly toward the stairs and down into the basement. What greeted her was shocking.

A small prison with four doors, two of which had padlocks on them. She could smell urine and it made her gag.

"In there."

She began to cry and turned toward

him.

"Please don't do this."

He got behind her, grabbed the cuffs around her wrist, and forced her to follow him backward into the cell. Pushing her to the floor, he looped and padlocked a chain around her leg before removing her original restraints. The door shut and a lock snapped. His steps retreated up the stairs, then nothing, just quiet.

"Who are you?"

A female voice from the next cell broke the silence, startling Suzanne. She leaned as close to the wall as she could.

"Suzanne. Who are you?"

"Chelsea. The man next to me is Ed. Do you know why he brought you here?"

"No. I was at home, and next thing I know, I'm in a van with a hood on my head. Do you?"

Suzanne could hear Chelsea start to sob.

"No. He won't tell us."

"How long have you been here?"

"A couple days. Ed's been here four."

"Has he hurt either of you?"

"No. Not yet."

Suzanne heard a man's voice from

the far cell.

"What did you say you're name is?"

"Suzanne."

"Suzanne what?"

"Suzanne Cooper."

"Is that your maiden name?"

"Yes, why?"

Ed ignored the question.

"Chelsea, is Morris your maiden name?"

Chelsea tried to stop crying.

"No. Burt...my maiden name was Burt."

Silence fell over the three of them as the girls waited to find out what Ed was driving at.

"Mother of God!"

"What?" Both girls asked in unison.

"Does the name 'Billy Jarvis' mean anything to either of you?"

****

It was near closing at the local dollar store, and Curt was finishing the last of the busywork.

"Wendy, I'm taking trash out; back in a minute."

"Okay."

He unlocked the back door and

carried the two bags to the dumpster. After throwing them in, he turned to go back, and noticed a teal-colored car parked at an odd angle. The dome light was on and the back door open. He didn't recognize the car, and everyone who worked at the plaza parked in the outer lot up front.

Curt walked down toward the vehicle and looked in. The keys dangled from the ignition, but the car wasn't running. Standing up, he looked around. He was alone in the back alley. He pulled out his cell phone.

****

Two uniformed officers responded to Curt's call. One was calling in the license plate, and the other was getting the final details of how Curt found the car.

The first got off the radio.

"Car belongs to a Suzanne Cooper. Address is not far from here."

"Get a phone number?"

"Yes. I'm trying it now."

The second officer turned back to Curt.

"Thanks for your help. You can go now; sorry to keep you so long."

"No problem."

As the dollar store employee walked away, the first officer hung up the phone.

"Answering machine."

"Okay, call in for a car to go by the address, and I'll get a tow truck to come take the car."

By the time the officers heard no one was answering at the residence, the car was on the truck and ready to go. Instead of the impound lot, it was sent to the forensics garage.

****

Ed Garland could hear both girls suck in their breath. Neither said anything, and Ed waited while it sunk in. He had already figured out the connection, all three of them had been there the day Billy Jarvis had shot himself playing Russian roulette.

The thing he hadn't figured out was their captor's identity. Finally, Chelsea spoke. "Ed, Ed Garland from McCollum High?"

"Yes."

"And Suzanne Cooper, Billy Jarvis's girlfriend?"

Suzanne didn't answer

immediately, but Chelsea could hear her crying.

"Suzanne?"

"Ye…yes."

"You're Billy's ex-girlfriend?"

"Yes."

"That means Dexter Hughes…"

Ed slammed his hand on the wall. "That's his name! I was sitting here trying to remember the other guy who was there that day. That's gotta be who the last cell is for."

Suzanne had regained her composure.

"If you're right, and Dexter is put in the last cell, then what? And who is the guy doing this?"

Ed's answer chilled them all.

"I don't know *who* he is, and I don't *want to know* what's next."

Chapter 13

Jason received a call the next morning from Lieutenant Banks.

"Go see Doc Josie when you get here."

"Okay. What's up?"

"You would have me ruin the surprise? I wouldn't think of it."

The phone went dead. Jason called Nina, who was just leaving the house. "Hello?"

"Morning, Nina. You heading in?"

"Yeah, why?"

"Banks called. She said we need to go see Doc Josie first thing; I'll meet you there."

"Okay. She say why?"

"Nope. Said it was a surprise."

"A surprise? Okay, see you in about twenty minutes."

****

Jason found Dr. Jocelyn Carter staring through a microscope.

"Morning, Doc."

She pulled her head back, rolled her eyes, and went back to the scope with a chuckle. "Maybe for you, Detective. For me, it's more like afternoon. Got a call at midnight to come in and process a car."

"Sorry to hear that."

Nina came through the doors and joined them. Jason stopped her before she had a chance to wish Doc Josie a good morning. "She's been here all night."

"Oh. Did you find out what the surprise is?"

"I was just about to ask. So Doc, is this car you mentioned our surprise?"

Doc Josie got off the stool and walked to her office with the detectives in tow. Grabbing a sheet of paper, she handed it to Jason.

"If this set of prints is what you're referring to, then yes, this is your surprise. Those partial prints were found on the car."

Jason gave her a quizzical look. "Let me guess. You've seen them before."

"Very good. You should be a detective."

Nina couldn't help herself and started laughing. Doc Josie continued.

"Not only have I seen them before, I've seen them recently. They match the ones we pulled from the two missing persons cases you're working."

Jason looked up from the print sheet. "Who does the car belong to?"

"A Suzanne Cooper. It was found abandoned, keys still in the ignition, behind a plaza near her home last night. Lieutenant Banks said they haven't been able to find Miss Cooper."

Nina walked over to a table, put her briefcase down, and popped it open. After rummaging for a minute, she pulled some papers out. "What was that name again?"

"Suzanne Cooper."

Jason watched as his partner ran her finger down the sheets. She stopped on the second page. "It's here, Jason."

"Are those the McCollum reunion lists?"

"Yes, and she's on them."

Jason moved for the door as Nina packed up. "Thanks, Josie. Go home and get some sleep."

"You're welcome, and I plan on doing just that."

****

Lieutenant Banks was in her office when they got to the second floor.

"Got a minute, Lieutenant?"

"Sure. Find your surprise?"

"Yes. Do you have the report from the scene?"

She slid the file across the desk.

Nina followed Jason into the room and sat next to him opposite the lieutenant. Jason picked up file, but didn't open it.

"We've got a connection between the three missing cases, besides the fingerprints."

"Okay. Please fill us in."

Nina pulled out the phone lists and slid them across the desk toward Banks. She picked them up, glanced at them, and then up at Nina. "What are these?"

"Those are the phone lists for this summer's ten-year class reunion of McCollum High. All three of our victims are listed on them."

The lieutenant looked at them with a disbelieving stare.

"You're suggesting someone is stalking, then taking their classmates before the reunion. You're kidding me, right? It sounds like a slasher film."

Jason shrugged his shoulders.

"I know it's thin, but right now it's the only link we've found."

"Thin is one word for it. What's next?"

"We run a record search on everyone listed."

"So, you're thinking the person or persons taking these people, or at very least possibly the next victim, are on these lists."

Jason nodded. The lieutenant stared at the sheets for a minute. "When's the reunion?"

"The fifth of next month."

"Okay. I'm going to have a press briefing on this at three this afternoon. We'll see if the public can help us. Somebody must've seen something. I want you two present. In the meantime, that's a lot of names, so you better get started."

Jason and Nina gathered their files and left the office. Nina gave Jason a grin. "Press briefing with Banks. Boy that sounds like fun!"

Jason just laughed and rolled his eyes.

****

Chelsea was cold. The basement was damp, and the blanket didn't give much protection. In addition, the chain was rubbing her ankle raw. She had spent the last several hours trying to figure out who their captor was.

"Suzanne?"

"Yeah."

"I think the guy doing this has to be related to Billy."

"Why?"

"Well, it doesn't make sense for someone to go to all this trouble without a personal connection."

Ed agreed. "I've been thinking the same thing. Billy was my best friend, but I don't remember much about his family. His dad was dead by the time of the accident, and I think he had only his mom and brother."

Suzanne's memories were the same. "The whole time I knew Billy, I only heard him talk about two people. His brother and his mom. I think the brother's name was Ronnie...Lonnie. Something like that."

Ed remembered. "Donnie. His brother's name was Donnie."

Chelsea pulled her blanket tighter around her. She wasn't feeling well. She had vomited once a few hours earlier, and it had just added to the stench surrounding them.

"That has to be it, she said. "It must be the brother. How old was he when Billy died?"

She could hear Ed rolling over before he answered, his chain scraping the floor. "Eleven or twelve, I guess. I'm not sure. I don't even see how knowing who he is helps us. In fact, it may make it worse."

The basement went quiet again. Knowing who their captor was should have helped, but it didn't. In fact, it made him all the more dangerous if he found out they knew.

Chelsea could now guess at what Donnie had in mind, and she didn't like it.

Chapter 14

Jason looked at his watch. Four hours of poring over the files of the three missing persons, and still no hint at who might be taking them. Nina was equally engrossed in the phone records, and when she looked up at him, her red eyes told the story. They needed a break.

"Two hours to the press conference. Want to get something to eat?"

Nina stretched out and groaned. "Definitely."

"Want to bring the phone records?"

"Definitely not!"

****

They got back with twenty minutes to spare. Lieutenant Banks was waiting for them.

"Let's go, you two."

The three of them rode down to the first floor together. When they came out of the elevator, a small group of reporters was waiting for them in the briefing room.

In its early days, the room had been the patrol prep room, but that was done elsewhere now. The department hadn't spent any money to make the press corps comfortable. It was still just desks and white concrete walls.

Devin James gave a nod to Jason, followed by a big smile for Nina. When Sarah Banks came into the room behind them, Jason saw the reporter's face go immediately blank. Jason smiled to himself.

Is everybody afraid of this woman?

Jason and Nina stood at the back of the small stage, the only addition to the room, as the lieutenant walked to the podium.

"Thank you for coming. We are investigating the disappearance of three people in the San Antonio area. The cases appear to be connected, and we're seeking the public's help."

On a screen behind the lieutenant, three photographs popped up.

"The first is Ed Garland, 28. The second is Chelsea Burt-Morris, age 28. Last night, a third person went missing. Her name is Suzanne Cooper, age 29."

Devin James stood up. "What's the connection between them?"

Lieutenant Sarah Banks did something Jason had never seen before. She ignored the senior reporter from the San Antonio News. But what really surprised Jason, was when James sat down without a fuss. Lieutenant Banks carried on where she left off.

"All three have gone missing in the last six days. We're asking the public to let us know if they have seen any of these people. We've set up an eight hundred number for people to call if they have any information on the whereabouts of these individuals."

She paused, and Jason expected James to try his question again, but he stayed seated.

"The lead investigators on this case are Detective Strong and Detective Jefferson. I will let them answer any questions you might have."

With that, the lieutenant stepped back and motioned for Jason and Nina to step up. Jason looked out over the group. "Questions?"

Devin James stood again, and asked the same question. "How are the three connected?"

"First of all, in all three cases,

we've found fingerprints from the same individual. We do not have an ID on this person yet, but we believe the prints belong to the perpetrator. Also, we have phone records from all three of the missing persons, and there is a number that connects them."

A different hand went up. "What's the number?"

"I'm sorry, but I can't reveal that."

James was still standing. "Do the three know each other?"

"We don't know. It's possible, but we're unable to say for sure."

Nina stepped forward. "I have a handout, with the full description of each person and the location they were taken from. It will be on the table by the door."

Lieutenant Banks, moving so swiftly she caught Jason by surprise, leaned in to the microphone. "That'll be all. Thank you for coming."

And the briefing was over.

Jason didn't like these things and treated them as a necessary evil, but he was impressed with the way Sarah Banks handled it. In the elevator, he said so.

"Short and sweet, my kind of press briefing."

Lieutenant Banks gave him a half smile. "Give 'em what you want them to have, then go back to work."

Jason thought it might be the best philosophy for dealing with the press he'd ever heard.

****

As the senior writer at the San Antonio News, Devin James could have a glass-paned office and a walnut desk, but he'd turned the perk down every time it was offered. He'd kept the same heavy schoolteacher-looking desk he got when he moved to crime duty more than twenty-five years ago.

Whenever they would offer him a new office, Devin would politely decline, saying he preferred the bustle of the pressroom. Truth was he didn't like the idea of being inside a 'glass cage,' as he referred to the offices.

He pulled up the rolling chair that matched the age of the desk and got out his notes from the briefing. Something was nagging at the back of his brain, and he couldn't get it to come out. He knew if he were patient, it would eventually make its way to where he could remember it. Unfortunately, it was taking longer these days to reveal those nagging thoughts in his memory.

Devin's attachment to antiques ended with the desk. He bought himself a new computer every year, and this year's model was a very nice Dell laptop. He turned it on, waiting briefly for it to boot up, and began writing the story from the briefing.

As he typed out the three names, he couldn't shake the feeling he knew them. It was as if he'd done this story before, where he'd typed these names out together. He stopped what he was doing and pulled up the search window for the San Antonio News archives. After typing in all three names, he hit the search button.

In just a few seconds, a story James had written over ten years ago popped up.

The Billy Jarvis suicide. I knew those names were connected somehow.

The reporter began to read his story, and some of the details started to come back. He remembered showing up at the house in the north San Antonio neighborhood after hearing a scanner report.

It was a tragic scene, and it stayed with him for a long time. A screaming mother, crying neighbors, and the feeling it was all so senseless.

As he went through the article, the

three names he'd searched stood out in bold print, but there was a fourth name. Dexter Hughes. He was also there that day. If the three missing were connected by the suicide, it could mean Hughes would be next.

Devin opened up a phone book, and ran his finger down the large number of Hughes listed in the San Antonio area. There was no guarantee the man still lived in the city, but the first three people missing had all remained local, maybe Hughes was also still around.

There was over eighty Hughes listed with the initial 'D.' Most were eliminated by the entire first name being listed, but James was still left with seven names.

He began dialing, and hoped Dexter Hughes didn't have an unlisted number.

Four numbers later, no luck. Number five was an answering machine.

"You've reached Dex, Trish, and the boys. Leave a message."

Devin hung up. He checked the address matching the fifth number. It was in West San Antonio.

Next, he got up, and went to the file cabinet behind his desk. In it, Devin kept the files containing his notes from every story he'd ever covered. It took some digging, but in short order, he found the file marked 'Jarvis Suicide.'

Taking it back to his desk, he opened it up, and read what he'd jotted down ten years before. He was looking for any mention of family of Billy Jarvis. If the disappearance of these people was tied to the death of Billy Jarvis, it made sense to him a family member would be responsible. He hoped he had the names of Billy's relatives in the file.

Eventually, he found a reference to the family. Billy had a father who was already dead, his mother was named Betty Jarvis, and a younger brother.

James went back to the phone book. He knew this time he was looking for a woman who may have remarried and no longer had the same last name.

James found the last name Jarvis had far fewer listings than Hughes, and only ten with first names starting with B. One listing said Betty. He dialed the number.

"Hello?"

"Hello. Is Betty Jarvis there, please?"

"Who's calling?"

"My name is Devin James. I'm a reporter for the San Antonio News."

"She's not here. Can I give her a

message?"

"Yes. Could you ask her to call me?"

"Sure."

James gave the man his phone number and hung up.

****

Donnie put the phone down and stared at it. The call scared him. He still had one person left to capture. The last thing he needed was a reporter calling and asking questions.

He'd watched the news on TV earlier and had seen the story about the missing people. The same ones he had in his basement.

It was clear he needed to move faster.

Chapter 15

Devin James decided to go past the Hughes house on his way home. He'd called again, and got the answering machine again. He wanted to stop by, check his theory, and then alert the police. After all, he had nothing but his suspicion to suggest anything might be wrong at the Hughes home.

He turned the corner onto their street, and discovered the house numbers in this neighborhood were on the brick mailboxes by the street. He followed the numbers down the road until he came to the Hughes. The house was a large, two-story brick home with dramatic dormers on the second floor and an immaculate lawn. Two trees, the ones you trim into odd shapes, stood guard on each side of the black front door.

There was a car in the driveway with the trunk open. A tall, dark-haired woman in a pantsuit was handing bags of groceries to two children. She grabbed the last bag herself, shut the trunk, and walked toward the house.

James parked and got out, moving across the lawn toward the door. "Mrs. Hughes?"

She stopped and turned to the reporter. "Yes?"

"My name is Devin James; I'm a reporter for the San Antonio News. Is your husband home?"

"I don't think so, Mr. James. His car's not here. Why are you asking?"

"I'm doing research for a story, and his name came up as a source for some background."

She continued up the walk and unlocked the door. The kids took their bags inside. "Oh. Did you call Dex at work?"

"No. I didn't have the number."

"If you'll wait a minute, I'll get it for you."

"That would be great."

She disappeared inside with her groceries, and a few minutes later, returned holding a business card.

"He's a sales rep for a billboard company. This is his card with his cell number."

James took the card and gave her one of his.

"If I don't reach him, would you have him call me?"

"Sure."

She closed the door, and James immediately started dialing while on his way back to his car.

"This is Dex Hughes with Barnaby Advertising. I'm sorry I missed your call. Please leave a message and I'll return your call as soon as I can."

James hung up and dialed the office number, also listed on the card.

"Barnaby Advertising."

"Is Dexter Hughes in?"

"No, sir. He's not been to the office today. Do you want his cell number?"

"No, thank you. I already have it."

Devin James hung up. What to do next? He needed to know the whereabouts of Dexter Hughes, but he didn't want to create panic based on a ten-year-old news story.

He started his car and looked at the address of Betty Jarvis. It was east of the city. He would pay her a visit in the morning.

****

Donnie slammed the door on the fourth cell and snapped the padlock shut. A quick look confirmed the other three cells were all still locked.

Tomorrow he would visit Billy one last time before completing the mission. Donnie wished Billy could be present to see the success of the plan, and he would love to be there when Billy received his final rest. Neither was possible, but it would be an exciting day anyway.

****

Dexter Hughes knew he wasn't alone. He had seen the other locked doors, and he could smell the stench of trapped humans. He jerked at his chain—it wasn't going to give—and looked around for an escape. He wasn't going anywhere, even if he did get loose.

"Dexter?"

He was startled to hear his name from the next cell. "Who's asking?"

"Suzanne Cooper. Are you Dexter Hughes?"

Dexter tried to place the name. He knew it, but from somewhere way in the past.

"Yes. Do I know you? How do you know me?"

131

"Well, that seals it."

This time it was a male voice, and it came from the far end of the room. A female started to cry.

"Can someone tell me what's going on?" Dexter asked.

The woman who had spoken first, her voice barely above a whisper, tried to explain. "The man in the far cell is Ed Garland. Next to me is Chelsea Burt. As I told you, I'm Suzanne Cooper. We guessed who you were because we all have a connection."

Dexter slumped back against the wall. "Billy Jarvis."

"That's what we think. Ed was taken first, Chelsea second, and me third. We knew if you were the one put in the last cell, all of this had to be connected to Billy."

"Who's the guy that's locked us in here?"

Ed spoke up from the far end. "Hey, Dex. Never thought I would speak to you again, especially under these circumstances. We think it's Donnie, Billy's little brother."

"But why?"

"We don't know, he won't answer us. Just keeps saying 'we'll find out soon.'"

"Have you told him you know who he is and that Billy wouldn't want him to do this?"

"No! We don't want him to know we've figured out who he is. We think it would just increase the danger."

Dexter tried to get comfortable on the blanket. "Makes sense, I guess. Not that any of this could make sense."

****

The next morning Devin James prepared to leave the house, but before he did, he called Dexter Hughes at home. A female voice answered. "Hello."

"Mrs. Hughes, this is Devin James with the newspaper; we spoke yesterday. Is your husband at home?"

"No. In fact he didn't come home last night."

"Is that unusual?"

"Yes, it's unusual!"

"I'm sorry, Mrs. Hughes. I didn't mean to offend. I think you should call the police."

"I already did, but they said it needed to be forty-eight hours before anything could be done."

"Do you have a pen and paper?"

"Yes."

"Call Detective Jason Strong. I know him, and he'll listen to you. You can tell him I gave you his name. Tell Detective Strong I believe your husband's disappearance may be tied to the cases he is working on."

"What cases?"

"I'm sorry, ma'am. I can't say more."

"Jason Strong?"

"Yes, ma'am."

"Okay. Thank you, Mr. James."

The phone went dead. James felt queasiness in his stomach. He hated when he was right about something like this; Dexter Hughes was missing.

Chapter 16

Donnie pulled up at 'Gates of Heaven' cemetery before sunrise. Today was the fulfillment of the plan he and Billy had been working on since that awful day ten years ago. Now they were finally going to make things right. It was going to be so sweet to see all their work pay off.

Donnie couldn't sleep, so he'd gotten up early and come to visit Billy for the last time before they played out the final step of the plan. Parking the van, he walked through the damp, morning grass to his big brother's grave. He felt a peace inside, a calm that came from knowing he had accomplished his task. The most important task his brother could ever give him. To bring him eternal rest.

"Good morning, Billy."

Donnie crouched down, listening intently.

"I know you're ready. I'm sure

135

going to miss our talks when you're gone."

Donnie smiled.

"Thanks. I did it all for you because you deserve it."

Donnie brushed the leaves off his brother's name.

"Don't worry about me, Billy. I don't think they know who I am, and if anyone survives, I'll make sure they don't know where to find me."

Donnie lingered by his brother for a little while. It reminded him of the visits he made with Momma when she was alive. They would just enjoy being together. But the events planned for this day would not allow Donnie to stay. Today was a day for action. "I've gotta go now, Billy."

Tears welled up in his eyes.

"I love you, too. You're the best brother a kid could ever have, and I'm gonna miss you."

He stood up.

"You're welcome. Tell Momma 'hi' when you see her. Make sure she knows I miss her."

Donnie hesitated a moment or two longer.

"Bye, Billy. I love you."

Donnie walked away with the usual

sadness, but now it was mixed with anticipation. He was coming to the end of a decade-long journey. He fired up the van and sped for home.

****

Jason arrived at work around his usual time. Waiting for him on his desk was a note.

Call Mrs. Hughes. Urgent. 555-230-4210.

Jason got himself a cup of coffee and sat down. He dialed the number.

"Hello?"

"Mrs. Hughes, please?"

"This is her. Is this Detective Strong?"

"Yes, ma'am. I had a note to call you?"

"Devin James, from the San Antonio News, he gave me your name. He said I should call you."

Jason did his best not to sound irritated, but he didn't like James using him as an inside contact. He would have to talk to him about it.

"Okay. What can I help you with?"

"My husband is missing."

"How long has he been gone?"

"I haven't talked to him since

yesterday morning, and his work said he'd never checked in."

"Well Mrs. Hughes, we don't consider an adult missing for at least..."

"Forty-eight hours, I know. Mr. James said you would help me. He said to tell you my husband's disappearance might be connected to some cases you're working on."

Jason had been leaning back in his chair with his legs crossed, but now he sat bolt upright and put down his coffee.

"Did he say what cases he was referring to?"

"I assume missing persons, but I'm not sure."

Nina came in and gave a nod before sitting down at her desk. Jason grabbed a pad.

"Mrs. Hughes, what is your husband's first name?"

"Dexter."

Jason wrote down Dexter Hughes.

"Okay. Can you hold on for a minute?"

"Sure."

Jason punched the hold button and gave the note to Nina. "Check and see if that name is on our reunion list."

Jason watched her intently as she scanned the sheets. It wasn't long before she looked up at him. "Yes. Dexter Hughes. Why?"

"I'll tell you in a minute."

He punched the hold button again. "Mrs. Hughes?"

"Yes."

"If you'll give me your address, my partner and I would like to come talk to you."

"Oh, thank you so much."

Jason wrote down the address and hung up. Nina was watching him, waiting for an explanation.

"I found a note on my desk this morning to call a Mrs. Hughes. When I called her, she said her husband was missing. Apparently, she has somehow got hooked up with Devin James, and he told her to call me."

"Oh, wasn't that nice of him!"

"Wait, there's more. James told her to tell me her husband disappearance was connected to the cases we're working on."

"You're kidding! How would he know that?"

"A very good question, one I intend to ask him as soon as I get a hold of him. Anyway, that's when you came in and confirmed the name on the list."

"So we're going over to talk to

her?"

"Yes, but first I have a call to make."

Jason picked up his phone and found the reporter's number in his contacts. He pushed 'call.'

"You have reached the phone of Devin James, crime reporter for the San Antonio News. Please leave a message and I will return your call as soon possible. Thank you."

Jason waited for the beep.

"Devin, this is Jason Strong. I received a call today from a Mrs. Dexter Hughes. Please call me; I have some questions for you. Thanks."

He hung up and looked at Nina. "Ready to ride?"

"Of course."

****

Devin James recognized the phone number of Jason Strong and let it go to voice mail. He figured Jason had talked to Mrs. Hughes and would have questions James wasn't prepared to answer. He would call Jason back when he got a handle on the situation at the Jarvis farm.

The reporter turned down the gravel

lane leading up to the farmhouse. He could see a van parked by the front porch, but no sign of anyone moving around outside. He crossed an old cattle guard and slowed to a stop next to the van.

Devin shut his car off, reached for the door handle, and froze. A young man surprised him at his side window.

He was maybe twenty, tall and thin, with dark eyes. James wasn't sure where he'd snuck up on him from. Perhaps he was in the van.

Devin rolled the window down and felt the blast of the late morning heat. The boy appeared tense. "You lost?"

James put on his best reporter's smile. "No, I don't think so. I wanted to talk to Betty Jarvis. Is she here?"

"Nope. She's gone to town. Are you the reporter who called the other day?"

"Yes. Are you Donnie?"

"Maybe. Is there something I can help you with?"

The boy stayed close enough to the door as to prevent Devin from opening it. Only by pushing him out of the way, could the reporter get out.

"I'm investigating the disappearance of four people. I wanted to ask your mother about it?"

"Momma doesn't know nothin' about no missing people."

"I'd like to ask her myself. Will she be back soon?"

"I told you she doesn't know nothin', and I don't know when she'll be back. I'd like you to leave now."

"I don't mind waiting."

"I said you need to leave!"

A gun appeared from behind the boy, and James didn't want a confrontation he would obviously lose, so he hurriedly rolled up his window. The young man watched him turn around, and continued to stare after him all the way down the lane.

James didn't turn right, the direction he'd come from, but went left instead. He'd seen a row of trees running across the back of the Jarvis property, and he thought they would serve as cover while he waited for Mrs. Jarvis to return.

Sure enough, he was able to pull off the road into the shade of an oak tree, and watch the house from a distance. He reached into the glove compartment and got out his binoculars. His instincts told him it wasn't a time for action, but a time for waiting.

Waiting and watching.

****

Donnie watched until the reporter had turned at the end of the lane. He felt very uneasy. The timing of the visit couldn't have been worse. Today of all days needed to go smoothly, and unexpected visitors were not part of the plan.

He turned and walked back to the house. He had preparations to finish and sensed his time was getting short.

Chapter 17

Jason and Nina pulled up at the Hughes house forty-five minutes later. Mrs. Hughes opened the door before the detectives could ring the bell. "Detective Strong?"

"Yes, ma'am. This is my partner, Detective Jefferson. May we come in?"

"Of course."

She let them in, and after closing the door, she guided them through an oak-paneled hallway, which opened up into an expansive kitchen. White cabinets, black granite countertops, and stainless steel appliances. It was right out of a magazine.

"Would either of you like coffee?"

Jason shook his head. "Not for me."

Nina also shook her head no and pulled out a chair from the kitchen table. Jason sat with her while Mrs. Hughes grabbed the coffee cup she had been using, refilled it from the pot, and joined them. As she held her cup, Jason noticed the shaking of what he guessed were normally steady hands.

Nina opened a notepad while Jason turned his chair to face the elegant woman. "Mrs. Hughes…"

"Please, call me Barbara."

"Barbara. I assume you haven't heard from your husband since we last spoke, is that right?"

"That's right. I keep trying his cell phone, and checking with his office, but there's no answer. They haven't heard from him either."

"Do you have a picture of your husband?"

"Yes, of course."

Barbara Hughes left the room and returned with a photo frame. She slid the picture out of the frame and handed it to Jason. Jason took a look before giving it to Nina.

Barbara followed it with her eyes almost as if it might be the last time she saw the image of her husband. Jason felt for the woman, and his frustration at not being able to tie everything together was starting to eat at him.

"Barbara, had your husband mentioned his upcoming class reunion?"

Jason could see the surprise on her

face.

"Yes. About a week ago. Does that have something to do with him missing?"

"We're not sure. The other cases we're working, the ones Devin James mentioned to you, are from the same high school class as your husband. We think it's likely there's a connection. When we found your husband's name on the class list, we came to see you without waiting the forty-eight hours."

"How many cases are there?"

"There are three others that we're aware of."

"Three! My husband is the fourth?"

"Yes, ma'am. Had your husband mentioned being concerned about the reunion, or being contacted by someone he wasn't comfortable with?"

Mrs. Hughes was still clearly trying to get a grasp on the thought her husband was one of four missing people. Her answers took on a robotic feel, as if she'd gone to autopilot.

"No. The only thing he said was the school had called to give him the date and place of the reunion."

Nina looked up from her note taking.

"Mrs. Hughes…"

"Barbara, please."

"I'm sorry...Barbara. We would like to access your husband's phone records, and it would be much faster if you just requested them for us."

"Of course. I'll call our provider now."

The tall brunette got up and left the room.

Jason looked at Nina.

"What do you think?"

"Four people from the same school, same class, and all in a week. We've got somebody who has a bone to pick."

"Yeah, but how many? This is four, how many more could there be?"

"Until we find the connection, the phone list is the only thing we have. There must be a smaller list, not all one hundred-plus classmates can be targets, and we need to figure out what that smaller list is. There must be something connecting these four that doesn't connect the rest of the class."

Barbara Hughes came back into the room.

"They're e-mailing the record from our last bill to me now. Here are last month's."

Nina took the sheets and they stood. Barbara Hughes walked back out of the room and, in less than a minute, came back with one more printed sheet.

She escorted them back to the front door and opened it for the two detectives. When Jason had stepped outside, he turned to face Mrs. Hughes. Jason looked into the woman's eyes and saw a pain there he recognized.

She wasn't whole. A part of her was missing and her life was out of balance, like a teeter-totter with no one on the other end. She couldn't make it move, couldn't do it alone. The fear she might have lost her partner in life visibly weighed on her, and Jason's heart ached for her.

"Barbara, we'll do everything we can to find your husband. Hang in there and we'll be in touch."

Tears started to well up as the stress began to come out the only way she knew how.

"Thank you, Detectives. I appreciate it."

As the door closed, Jason's face turned hard.

"We need to find the animal taking these people, and fast!"

****

Devin James had waited long

enough. There was no movement around the farm, but something wasn't right and he could feel it.

While he was sitting and watching, he had planned a route he thought would get him up near the buildings without being seen. If he stayed in the tree line until the garage hid him from the house, he might be able to run up without Donnie knowing he was there. He didn't want another confrontation with the gun.

Betty Jarvis hadn't shown up from town, and James was beginning to suspect she didn't live there at all. That, or something had happened to her.

He made his mind up it was time to move, but before he left the vehicle, he dialed San Antonio police headquarters.

"SAPD."

"Yes, is this Sergeant Connor?"

"Yes, sir. Who am I speaking with?"

"This is Devin James with the San Antonio News."

"Afternoon Mr. James, what can I do for you?"

"I want to leave a message for Detective Strong."

"Do you want me to see if he's in?"

"No, I don't have time. Can you just give him a note when you see him?"

"Sure. Let me get a pen…okay, shoot."

"Tell him to pull the file from the Billy Jarvis suicide. It's from ten years ago."

"Okay. Pull the Billy Jarvis file. Anything else?"

"Yes. Tell him it's connected with the missing persons."

"Got it."

James hung up before Sergeant Connor could ask any more questions. He took his binoculars and a small digital camera with him, locked the car door, and crawled under a barbed wire fence. Staying low, and avoiding a small herd of Texas Longhorn cattle, the reporter made his way along the fencerow behind the cover of the trees.

Five minutes brought him to the spot opposite the garage where he was hidden from the house. He paused and took out his binoculars, searching the property for Donnie. There was still no one moving around, and no sign he'd been spotted.

He watched for a full ten minutes, catching his breath, before moving again.

Climbing under the back fence to the Jarvis property, he stayed crouched, and made a run for the back of the garage.

****

Jason and Nina arrived back at the station and walked through the front doors.

"Jason!"

He turned to where he heard his name called, and saw his friend Dave Connor holding up a sheet of paper. Nina continued up the stairs while Jason walked over the sergeant's desk.

"Hi, Dave. How's things?"

"Good. You?"

"Not bad. What's the note?"

The sergeant handed the note to the detective.

"Your buddy Devin James called around a half-hour ago and left you a message."

"*Buddy* is not how I would normally describe him."

Jason read the note and his pulse quickened. He walked away without thanking Dave.

"You're welcome."

Jason turned. "Sorry. Temporarily distracted. Thanks, and say hi to Vicky for me."

"Will do."

Instead of going upstairs, Jason went to Records in the basement.

****

Marie Turley had been with SAPD for thirty-eight years. She had moved to Records after three years as a dispatcher, and her memory for cases had made her famous around the precinct. She could track down files and names better than anyone. At sixty-one, she was still sharp, and prided herself on keeping up with as many cases as she could.

The Records office could be lonely and was usually quiet, except for the country music Marie kept on the radio. Johnny Cash, Mel Tillis, or some other old country star was always filling the empty room.

Marie was busy with the regular duties of pulling requested files, and re-filing the ones they were finished with. Jason snuck up behind her and leaned over her shoulder.

"Boo!"

"Ahhh!" She clutched her heart. "You scared the crap out of me."

"Oh, good. Then I've accomplished something today."

"Very funny."

She smiled up at the detective. Most detectives tended to treat her like their personal librarian, but Jason Strong was not like most detectives. He treated her like family, and she was very fond of him. There wasn't any piece of information Jason could ask for that wasn't pushed to top of her list.

"Whatcha need, or did you just come down to brighten my day?"

"Not that doing so wasn't reason enough to visit. However, I do have a request."

"Anything for you, Sweet-cheeks."

Jason smiled back at her. She had called him that since he first joined the force as a rookie cop.

"I'm looking for the file on a suicide case. The name is Billy Jarvis."

"Oh, I remember that. About ten years ago. Very sad. I believe he was about eighteen."

"You're amazing, Marie. Can you find it for me?"

"I'll do my best. Give me some time, and I'll call you when I locate it."

"You're the best. Thanks."

Marie had already turned away as the detective headed out of her office. She loved these kinds of requests. They tested her memory and challenged her

For My Brother

ability to locate old files. She was deeply involved in the hunt before the door had even closed behind Jason.

Chapter 18

Devin James pressed his back up against the garage wall. At fifty-eight, he was in decent shape, but dashing across an open field while trying to stay low was the kind of physical test he wasn't used to. He leaned on the building and sucked air, waiting for his pulse to slow. He still hadn't seen any movement.

Finally able to focus, the reporter crept to the edge of the garage and peered around the corner. The house was about two hundred feet from where he stood. Backtracking to the other corner, he leaned to where he could see the front yard. The van was still in the same place.

Devin's breathing had returned to normal and it was time to move. He made a quick dash to the rear wall, ducking below a window. Again, he stopped and listened. He heard voices, but couldn't tell where they were coming from.

Slowly lifting his head, he looked

over the edge of the windowsill into a living room. No one was in the room, and the TV wasn't on. He crouched back down, and tried to make out what was being said. Despite his best efforts, all he could hear were muffled words.

On his knees now, Devin crawled the length of the house and looked around the corner. From there he could see a window into the basement. The voices had gotten a little louder, but there was no other movement. Staying on his knees, he crawled the fifteen feet to the window well. Looking through, it took him a minute to figure out what he was seeing.

The reporter found himself staring at some sort of a makeshift prison: cell doors with padlocks. He tested the window, and it gave slightly. A pungent odor wafted from inside, and the talking stopped. Then everything went black.

****

Donnie put down the slab of wood and stared at the reporter.

This changes everything. He knows where I live and who I am. Billy didn't say anything about what to do if someone caught on to the plan.

He reached down and dragged Devin James away from the window. Taking a zip tie, he crossed the man's hands behind his back, slipped the tie over them, and pulled it tight.

The reporter gave a slight moan. There was blood oozing from the back of the reporter's head, but Donnie was relieved to find out he hadn't killed the man. As James started to come around, Donnie grabbed his tied hands and forced him to his feet.

"Move!"

"Where...where are you taking me?"

"Just move."

Donnie steered the reporter into the garage and to the back wall, forced him to sit down, and pulled out another zip tie. He wrapped it around James's legs and cinched it tight. Satisfied the reporter wasn't going anywhere, Donnie turned to leave.

"Why are you doing this?"

Donnie turned and studied Devin James. He found himself longing to tell someone. To talk to someone about the plan beside his brother, but he didn't think there was anyone he could trust. The reporter already knew who Donnie was and might try to understand.

"Because I have to."

"Why? Does it have to do with Billy?"

The mention of his brother's name made him pause. James may have figured things out, and maybe Donnie could share with him. The moment passed, and he realized this was wasting valuable time.

Donnie walked over to a shelf, picked up a roll of duct tape, and wrapped a strip completely around the reporter's head, covering his mouth.

"You ask too many questions for your own good."

Donnie left the garage, closing the door behind him, and went to the front porch. Sitting in the same chair where he'd found Momma dead less than a week ago, he weighed his options. He had a decision to make.

I don't know who the reporter might have told about me. For all I know, the cops are on their way. There's two choices. Abandon the plan and get as far away from here as I can. Or go through with it and risk being caught.

He sat looking out over the farm for a long time, but he knew he had to get moving, and he knew he only had one choice.

He got up and went into the house.

****

Jason had just got to his desk when the phone rang. He hadn't even sat down yet. "Strong."

"Jason, this is Marie. I found your file."

"Fantastic. Be right down."

Nina watched him turn and head back toward the door.

"Where are you going?"

"Back to Records, Marie found my file."

"What file?"

"Back in a minute."

With that, he was gone.

****

Donnie cleared off the kitchen table and pulled back the chairs. He had planned to pull the drapes and shut the front door to keep his captives from knowing where they were. With the reporter showing up, there wasn't any point in trying to hide the location. He still didn't know if they had figured out who he was, so that would remain secret. Opening the basement door, he headed down the stairs.

It was time to set things up.

****

Jason returned to the office with a file in his hand and walked around to Nina's side of the desk. Laying it out in front of her, he pointed at what he'd found.

"Ed Garland, Suzanne Cooper, Chelsea Burt, and Dexter Hughes."

"All four?" She flipped the file closed to look at the name on the front. "What is this?"

"It's the report on a suicide from ten years ago involving a kid named Billy Jarvis."

"Okay, what's the connection to our missing persons?"

"They were all there. They were witnesses. Apparently, they took part in a game of Russian roulette with Jarvis. Jarvis shot himself while these four watched."

"How did you find this?"

"You know the message Dave Connor waved at me when we came in?"

"Yeah."

"It was from Devin James. He told me to look up this file."

"But how did he know?"

"If I had to guess, I'd say he did the story."

"So what now?"

Jason took the file back, sat at his desk, and opened it to a different page.

"The only names listed in the file besides the four witnesses are the mother, Betty Jarvis, and the younger brother, Donnie. Let's start there. I'll try to locate the mother, you see if you can find the son."

"You think a family member is responsible?"

"Isn't that usually the case?"

Nina nodded.

"Usually."

****

Ed Garland had heard each of the others sharing the basement prison with him being removed from their cells, one by one. First Dexter, followed by Suzanne, and then Chelsea. Each time, a lock would snap open, a door would complain with a grind as it swung wide, followed by the sound of chain dragging on the concrete. He'd heard both girls start to cry, but nobody had said anything to Donnie.

Within a few minutes, he would hear two sets of footsteps going up the stairs. He knew he was next, and now he heard the lock on his own door snap open.

The door swung wide, and the bare light bulb on the ceiling temporarily blinded him. He felt something hit his leg, and when he looked down, a set of handcuffs was lying next to him.

"Put 'em on."

Ed was weak, and didn't have the strength to argue. He clicked one wrist, then the other, into the cuffs. Next, something else was thrown at him. A key.

"Unlock the chain."

He did, fumbling with the lock because of the cuffs. When the lock snapped open, he unwrapped the chain from around his leg to expose raw, bleeding skin. The removal of the chain sent instant pain shooting up his leg as air hit the open wound.

"Get up, come out here."

Ed hadn't stood fully erect in nearly a week, and it was painful to try. Finally, he made it all the way up, but could only limp on the one good leg. Making his way to the door, he limped out of the cell he'd occupied for nearly seven days.

Donnie Jarvis stood there, gun in hand, gesturing toward the steps. Ed did his best to keep moving forward. Leaning on the wall as he made his way up the steps, he climbed slowly to the kitchen.

His captor seemed content to let Ed take his time. Donnie didn't push him or say anything to hurry Ed up. Just followed with the gun raised toward Ed's back.

When Ed got through the door into the kitchen, he started to shake. He didn't know if it was from the effort of getting up the stairs or from the sight that greeted him when he got there. Probably both.

Sitting in three chairs were his three cellmates. It was the first time he'd seen any of them, and they didn't look any better than he did. Both girls had tears running down their faces, and Dexter looked terrified. No one spoke.

The gun pushed into his back. "Over there, sit."

Ed thought about making a run for the door, but he knew he was in no shape to do so. He wouldn't get ten feet, so he limped around to the chair and sat.

Donnie came up behind him, put a zip tie around his elbow, and pulled it tight to the chair's arm. He repeated it on the other arm.

Donnie then stood back against the cellar doorframe and slowly looked from one person to the next; studying each for something Ed couldn't guess. When he'd made his way around the table, Donnie opened the gun, and took all the bullets out of the rotary chamber. He then stood them one by one in the center of the table.

When he was finished, he picked up the first bullet in the line-up, and shoved it back into the gun. He snapped the chamber shut and spun it.

"Time to play."

John C. Dalglish

Chapter 19

Jason and Nina each started with a criminal records search on their Jarvis, and both came up empty. Nina was the first to move on to a driver's license search, and she got a hit.

"Donald Jarvis. Age twenty-two. Gives an address east of the city."

Jason shook his head. "Apparently Betty Jarvis doesn't have a current driver's license."

He grabbed the phone book on the corner of his desk and looked up Betty Jarvis. He flipped the book around so Nina could see it. "Is that the address on the son's license?"

Nina compared them. "Yes."

Jason was immediately on his feet. "Let's go."

****

Donnie decided to have the girls

play last. He walked around to the back of Dexter Hughes's chair and spun the chamber of the gun once more. Hughes started to whimper. Donnie did his best to remain detached.

It had to be done. For his brother.

"I've brought you all together to finish the game you started with Billy Jarvis. Each of you is going to get the turn you didn't take ten years ago."

"Donnie, don't do this!"

It was Suzanne, and Donnie was startled to realize they knew who he was.

"So, you've figured out who I am. It doesn't change anything. Billy can only rest after the four of you have taken your turn."

It was his captives' turn to appear stunned, and Donnie could see it on their faces as the enormity of what was about to happen dawned on each one.

"You first, Hughes."

Donnie spun the chamber on the .38 revolver for a third time, pulled the hammer back, and placed it against the back of Dexter Hughes's head.

He pulled the trigger.

****

As Jason and Nina came out of the

elevator, Jason saw Dave Connor waving another note at him. He thought about ignoring it, but if it was from Devin, he wanted it. He looked at Nina. "Can you bring the car around? I need to see what Dave has for me."

"Sure."

She continued out the doors as Jason went over to the sergeant's desk. "Another note from James?"

"Not this time. Lieutenant Banks, she wants to see you."

Jason stopped short. He didn't want to lose time explaining everything to Banks. He left the note in Dave's hands.

"Tell her you tried to give it to me, but I was in too much of a hurry."

"You sure, buddy?"

"I'm sure. Thanks."

Jason turned and hurried out the doors to the waiting car. The lives of four people took priority now. He'd worry about Lieutenant Sarah Banks later.

****

Dexter Hughes sat in his chair shaking. The gun has only clicked.

"You win, Hughes. You don't die today."

Donnie stepped back from Dexter

Hughes and circled the table, every eye fixed on him. When he came around to the back of Ed Garland, he stopped.

"Don't do this, Donnie. You won't get away with it."

"At this point, I don't expect to get away with it, since you know who I am, but I do plan to get away. They won't find me."

Donnie spun the chamber again, a longer spin this time.

Again, he pulled back the hammer, and could feel more than see Ed Garland close his eyes. The girls both had theirs closed, as well.

Donnie laid the barrel against the back of Ed Garland's head and pulled the trigger.

Click!

Chapter 20

Nina had put her blue light on the top of the car and she used her horn at intersections. They were moving through traffic quickly, but Jason couldn't shake the feeling they were running out of time.

His phone rang, and it showed the lieutenant's cell phone. Jason decided he better pick up.

"Strong."

"This is Lieutenant Banks. I requested you in my office ten minutes ago. Where are you?"

"We're in the car."

He rolled his eyes at Nina.

"Don't play dumb with me, Detective. Why are you two not sitting in front of me right now?"

Jason sighed, and tried to come up with a short version of a long story.

"We have a lead on where the four missing persons might be."

"Four!"

Jason realized they hadn't yet told the lieutenant about Dexter Hughes.

"Uh, yeah. We discovered a fourth missing person who was tied to the same case."

"Nice of you to share."

"Sorry, Lieutenant. We felt a need to follow up immediately on this lead."

"Where are you? And don't say in the car."

"We're on our way to the home of Betty Jarvis and her son, Donnie."

"How did you get their names?"

This conversation just kept getting worse. Jason braced himself. "Devin James."

"The reporter!"

"Yes, ma'am."

"And how did he get onto them?"

"Apparently, he wrote a story some ten years ago that helped him make a connection."

A long silence on the other end, followed by a question that caught Jason by surprise.

"Do you need any backup?"

"As of yet, we don't know what we'll find. I'll call immediately if we need support."

"Very well, Strong. You'd better be right."

The phone went dead. Jason looked at his phone, then at Nina. "That went well."

****

Donnie pulled the gun away from the back of Ed Garland's head.

"Well Ed, it seems it's your lucky day also. You've played and won."

Ed said nothing, and Donnie thought the man may have passed out.

Donnie spun the chamber repeatedly, each rotation causing the girls to jump, as he walked around to the other side of the table. He stopped behind Chelsea Burt, continuing to spin the chamber as he stood there.

Chelsea began to sob uncontrollably. Donnie spun the chamber twice more and pulled back the hammer. He could tell the girl was saying something under her breath but could only barely make it out.

"Please no…please no….please…"

Donnie laid the gun against her skull, and the girl instinctively leaned away from him. He reached out and grabbed a chunk of her hair, pulled her back toward him, and squeezed the trigger.

****

Nina steered the car off I-10 and headed west toward the farm. They came to the address in just a few minutes. Kicking up a trail of dust, they sped up the lane toward the house. Jason could see no movement as they approached.

****

Click!

The sound caused Chelsea to jump, and she let out a whimper. Donnie stood back. Three had played and all three had won. Something began to gnaw at the back of Donnie's brain. Something he fought to suppress, to keep from distracting him. He chanted to himself to keep his focus.

Finish the job, finish the job, finish the job.

Feeling a growing anxiety, he hurried around behind Suzanne. Donnie had purposely chosen her last, hoping she might be spared. She had been Billy's girlfriend, and Donnie had known her well, even had a crush on her.

Now he stood behind her, and looking into the reflection on the china cabinet across the room, he could see the face of the last person to play the game. It now looked as if the odds were stacked against her, and he could see the realization in her eyes.

Suzanne was staring right back at him in the cabinet glass. Her eyes looked directly in to his, and she spoke to him as a friend.

"Donnie, you know me. You know this doesn't have to happen. You have the power to stop now, no one has died, and no one needs to die."

Donnie slowly shook his head. He knew he had to finish, or all this would be for nothing. He couldn't face the possibility that none of this accomplished its purpose, and for that to happen, Suzanne had to play.

He broke his eyes away from her stare, rolled the chamber three times, pulled back the hammer, and laid the gun against her head.

"No! Donnie, no!"

Her voice reverberated around the room as he pulled the trigger.

Click!

Donnie had braced himself for the gun to go off. Now his head spun from the silence. Nobody moved, Chelsea still sobbed but without making any noise.

Suzanne let out a sigh, and Donnie caught her look in the china cabinet. The relief on her face was obvious but Donnie also saw something else. Was it sadness for him?

Donnie stood there, the gun in his hand, and tried to make sense of what just happened.

All four played and no one died. Everything I've done to bring about this moment was for nothing. It hasn't changed anything. Billy is still the only one who is dead.

Donnie couldn't grasp the fact everything was over. He didn't feel relief, nor did he feel like he had accomplished something wonderful. The thought Billy might now be at rest did not help.

Donnie reached onto the table and picked up the five bullets still standing in the middle. One by one, he put them back into the gun's chamber. The eyes of everyone at the table grew wide.

But he didn't aim at anyone. Instead, he took the keys to the handcuffs and threw them on the table where the bullets had been. Everyone's focus went to the ring of keys while Donnie walked away, through the back door, and out to Momma's grave.

****

Nina stopped the car next to a van parked in front of the house. Both detectives got out. Nina took a quick look, cleared the van, and the two detectives walked onto the front porch. Jason knocked on the door.

"Help! Help us!"

Both detectives drew their guns, Nina pulled open the screen door, and Jason kicked the front door in.

"Police!"

When the two detectives came through the door, it took them a few seconds to let the scene before them sink in. It was clear their suspect was not in the room.

One of the girls screamed. "He went out back."

Jason looked toward the back door. "Is he alone?"

"Yes."

"Is he armed?"

"Yes."

"Is there anyone else in the house?"

"No, I don't think so."

Jason looked at Nina. "Call it in. I'm gonna see if I can find him."

Jason ran back out the front door.

For My Brother

Donnie stood at the foot of Momma's grave. Something wasn't right. He could feel it inside. He'd done everything Billy had told him, but nothing had changed. Billy was still the only one who died from playing the game. Donnie had put these people through all this, and nothing changed.

Donnie started to doubt the entire plan.

Maybe the whole purpose was revenge for his brother. Or maybe I'd never heard Billy at all. Was all this my own idea? Was it me who couldn't accept the death of Billy? Had I been the one who needed the others to play?

Despair washed over him as the questions weighed him down. He was alone now. No Billy. No Momma. No purpose.

Jason had just stepped off the front porch when he heard the explosion of a gun being fired. Still with his weapon drawn, he came around the side of the house but didn't see anybody. He ran up the side of the garage and stuck his head around the corner.

"Oh no!"

****

Nina heard the gunshot but didn't know where Jason was. She left the kitchen through the back door, crossing over to the side of the garage. She crept along the wall and peered around the corner.

Under a large oak tree, Jason was kneeling over a young man, his fingers pressed against the man's throat. He looked at Nina and shook his head.

A loud banging echoed from the garage wall. Both officers went to the back door of the garage, weapons drawn. Again, Jason kicked the door open, and the two rushed in. They trained their guns on the surprised face of Devin James.

For My Brother

Epilogue

Jason got off the elevator on the second floor. Lieutenant Banks had made it clear he was to stop by her office before going upstairs. He had taken a few days off after the Jarvis case, but he knew the time was coming when he would have to face Sarah Banks. That time was now.

She was sitting at her desk going over some paperwork when he knocked on the doorjamb. She looked up and removed her glasses.

"Come in, Detective. Shut the door behind you."

He closed the door but did not sit down. Instead, he leaned against the door he had just closed. He suspected it made him feel better to be close to an exit. She didn't waste time.

"I expect any detective working a case for me to make themselves available to me whenever I see the need. I also insist on being kept in the loop about the cases they have been assigned by me. I do not like being kept in the dark."

"Yes, ma'am."

"Having said that, I consider a detective's gut instinct to be his or her best tool in solving difficult cases."

Jason shifted from one foot to the other but didn't say anything.

"You followed your gut and put the victims ahead of a department protocol. As a result, lives were saved."

The lieutenant stood up and extended her hand.

"Excellent work, Detective Strong. And thank you."

Jason stepped forward and shook the lieutenant's hand. "Thank you, Lieutenant. I appreciate it."

Jason turned and left the office. On his way out, he saw Nina Jefferson sitting at a desk. He stopped.

"Hi, Nina. You finishing up the file on Jarvis?"

Nina looked up and gave Jason a sheepish grin. "Uh...no. That's done. Actually, Lieutenant Banks asked me to join her team, and I accepted."

Jason just stared at her for a minute, before breaking into laughter. "No kidding? Well, good luck."

"Thanks. I'm going to miss working with you."

Jason laid his hand on Nina's shoulder. "The feeling is mutual. See ya around, Detective."

"Bye, Jason. Tell Vanessa welcome back."

Jason rode the elevator up to Homicide on the third floor. When the doors opened, a familiar sight, one he'd been missing for awhile now, greeted him.

Detective Vanessa Layne sat at her desk reading a file. He walked up without her noticing. "Good morning."

She looked up and smiled at him.

"Hey, JD. How's it going this morning?"

"Fine. Just fine."

Author's Note

As I prepare to release the third novella in the Jason Strong series, I wish to say to all who have written me, how grateful I am to hear you have taken Jason and his crew into your life. It has been exciting for me to meet these characters, but even better to find out you like them as well.

"For My Brother" was by far the hardest story to write so far. In fact, this is the second time I've finished the book. The idea came together early on, and fairly quickly, but the sequence of events in the first writing didn't provide the book I had hoped for.

The first writing also did not provide the book my wife, Beverly, expected from me. Hence, the second writing. She had approved this one as I went along, and I trusted her instincts.

My friend, Mark, also felt the first writing did not measure up. So, the bottom line is, this book took much longer, and was much harder, than I had anticipated. I hope you find it worth the wait.

Feel free to contact me at (jdalglish7@gmail.com) or visit my website (jcdalglish.webs.com) Also, you can visit Jason at his Facebook page:

For My Brother

Thank You and God Bless, John
I John 1:9

CREDITS

Edited by Samantha Gordon, Invisible Ink Editing.
Cover by Beverly Dalglish

Made in the USA
Middletown, DE
13 March 2020